Prologue

Why is the beginning always the hardest? I have spent years debating the best way to start telling this story and none of the openings ever seemed adequate. Perhaps I will start with the cliché opening because it is the most efficient. Nothing you know is completely true, your Bibles, your records, your testaments, all a bit whitewashed and shifted to conform to a divine marketing plan. Sorry, but it's true. Who am I to speak such blasphemy? I am Remiel, one of the nine, not four, but nine Archangels. I, along with my brothers Raguel, Saraqael and Lucifer, were part of the divine restructuring plan that occurred. We made certain choices that made God, or Elohim as we called him, upset so he decided to remove our names from the books.

Ironically, you have to take it on faith that what I am saying is true. I am fully aware that I am asking you to take me on faith while telling you that what you have been taking on faith is wrong, hence the complications I have had starting this testament. Perhaps it is the prevalence of things I see on TV and in books scratching closer and closer to the truth that encouraged me to do this. It seems to me that perhaps humans are ready to listen, the Crusades and Inquisitions are long over, Rome has lost much of its political power. The fortunes of kings and countries no longer rise and fall with the Pope's decree.

You see, it was never supposed to be about God vs Lucifer. We never meant for whole doctrinal systems to be created about or around us. We were just doing a job really, creating worlds and galaxies. A family of beings created from the energy of the universe to organize it, provide structure and bring things to life. Then we had a family argument that no one wanted to give way on, Elohim insisted on creating things that worshiped him and

1

only him, Lucifer disagreed and if you'll forgive the pun, all hell broke loose.

I remember when we first came to this planet. We had been spending years creating life elsewhere. Every world is different and we had to learn the best ways to go about building ecosystems, as they came to be called. We didn't manifest knowing how to build a human from dirt, there was a bit of a learning curve involved. Elohim was the only one of us that could actually bring things to life. He always had an arrogant streak about that. The rest of us worked out the design flaws on something, we'd bring it to him, he'd give it life and we would see how it did or did not work. The original plan for any planet, including this one that we went to was to create life in several forms; let it evolve on it's own for a while, come back around some time later, tinker with it if need be, see what had evolved and then move on. So to settle the evolution vs intelligent design vs creation debate once and for all, all of you are correct.

There was never a "divine plan" other than to get things created, make sure planets didn't collide with each other when they weren't supposed to and keep things in harmony. We came to this planet, saw that it had a lot of the basics needed for an immense diversity of life to be put here so it became one of our favorite testing grounds for new ideas.

We decided to really see just how far assisted evolution could go. We started with all those single celled things and dropped by at regular intervals to see how things were going. We'd add new things to the mix, watch and learn. Not all of our designs were perfect and evolution did take some weird turns, we are fully responsible for some things though. The platypus and the T-rex, neither one makes any sense really. Who, in their right mind would create a huge reptilian predator with massive legs and jaws and incredibly useless arms? Divine entities who had been experimenting with fermentation that's who. Poor thing had an incredibly hard time eating what it killed. The platypus was sort of a joke. We didn't think Elohim would actually go for it, that's neither here nor there though.

Creating plants and animals became a bit tedious for some of us, especially Lucifer and Elohim. They wanted to create a being that could build and create things like we did. I pointed out in passing that many of the animals that existed already were building and creating things but he felt that they were inferior in design. Elohim wanted something that he could speak to directly and charge them with different tasks. Some of us had serious doubts about this idea as it seemed to run counter with creating harmony in the universe. It felt as if this new creation would be able to overpower everything else at some point in it's evolution and destroy what we had created to be in balance. Elohim and Lucifer felt that they could somehow program this new creation to not be destructive and started on the project. The rest of us went about our other tasks and left them to their project.

The original designs for what ultimately became humans were seriously flawed. It took them a long time to figure out how to make opposable thumbs work, the whole bipedal movement concept is much more complicated than you may think. Some of the early prototypes they let develop and that's where primates came from. They had to see how they moved and manipulated things to figure out how to improve upon the design. Finally they hit upon a design that worked. Elohim left it to Lucifer to handle all the aesthetic details and between the two of them they created the human that became known as Lillith, that's when the problems began and where our story truly begins.

CHAPTER 1

I can still vividly remember the morning they were going to bring her to life. Lucifer was literally glowing with excitement. She was a masterpiece, shimmering brown hair, green eyes, well proportioned, brown hued skin that was vibrant and soft. She wasn't overly tall but was finely boned and well muscled. Lucifer always made his creations just that extra touch more beautiful and delicately crafted, Lillith was no exception. She had been built to be strong, independent and creative, she was all that and more.

"Well brother, you have certainly outdone yourself." Elohim congratulated him.

"Thank you. Indeed I have. She needs to be more intelligent than the other animals if she is to build and create the way we want her to. She needs to be able to make her own decisions unimpeded." Lucifer had always been an advocate for humans to have free will. Elohim, not so much.

"We must put some limitations on her, her future mate and their offspring," Elohim pointed out, "They have to protect what we have made and understand that we gave them this so they always honor it."

"They will honor it brother. Look at how beautiful it is! Why wouldn't they?" Lucifer was also a bit idealistic and naive about things.

I spoke up, although I was perhaps the weakest one of my family we had always treated each other as equals. "Lucifer, I think he has a point. We are creating something that may be capable of completely restructuring this world. They have to have some understanding of balance and harmony."

"Not just that Remiel," Elohim spoke. "They need to understand their place in it. The animals, they instinctively know their roles, hunter or hunted, eater of waste, pollinator of plants, they know what their purpose is. We created them with a specific purpose in mind. This new creation has to know its role. We can't have it running about the place with no limits or ingrained path. It can do everything all the animals can do. It can hunt or be hunted, it may eventually learn how to cultivate plants if we allow it and build it's own habitat. It is not a creation that has a defined niche, it is fluid. We must make it fear something. It must know its place."

"Why does she have to fear us?" Lucifer's rebuttal began. "We can teach her balance and harmony and how to watch over this world without destroying it."

"Lucifer," Michael spoke up. He pretty much always sided with Elohim. "I agree with Elohim. Let's not unleash this new creation with no limits at all. If it works well we can adjust the mate to have less limits if needed."

Lucifer looked at us, his pale gold eyes piercing. Lucifer rightly deserved the title of Morningstar or the most beautiful of us. When he took what we called our "walking about form" his long hair matched that blinding, golden white color that shows only when the sun first crests over the horizon in the early morning. He stood taller than all of us and although his skin was pale his aura of power glowed sunset reds and purples. At the time, our auras were the only form of clothing we had. We are beings of energy, body awareness has never been a large concern of ours. We walked upright and had hands when we needed them, sometimes we took four footed or even winged forms. It depended on what we were doing at the time, sometimes we just switched form for fun.

Elohim was darker hued, his eyes were almost lavender in color, his hair was dark and short. He carried about him a sense of power that none of us ever matched, his fiery aura reflected the fires of creation, shifting in red-gold tones moment to moment. Michael was bronze and gold, he was the ultimate warrior even though there was no need for one that early on. He always had his red hair tied back and he had immense strength. His green eyes seemed hardened by battles that he had yet to fight. I've often wondered if somehow Michael had known what was yet to come and was preparing for it from the beginning of time.

"Brothers, why should we create something as wonderful as her and then hobble her?" Lucifer's rebuttal continued, "Why should we make the most exquisite and intricate thing we have ever made be forced to fear us? We have not made any other creature fear us. She can love us as we love each other can't she? When we create her mate they can love and protect each other and learn together as so many of the other creatures we have created do. When we first spoke of creating her we did it with the idea of making something as similar to us as possible. Obviously they will not be able to grant life or create animals from dust but if they are to be like us in other ways they should be treated as partners in this world they are to care for. Not as some lowly creatures that must bow before us. We don't bow to each other do we?" He paused and gestured to the rest of us. "I would never expect Remiel or Raguel or Uriel to bow to me even though I am stronger in some ways than they are. We are all the same family and all have our own skills and strengths. These new creations that are to be similar to us, are they not also family?"

I watched Elohim as Lucifer spoke. He was the only one that could bring our creations to life so he always had the final say when it came to what would and wouldn't be allowed to exist. The longer Lucifer spoke the more frustrated Elohim seemed to get.

"Lucifer!" Elohim's voice crackled, he seemed offended by the idea that a creation we made could be family. "You have, as usual, become too attached to your creations. You and I have both worked on this new creation, I wish it to thrive as you do but it is something we give life to. It is not born of the universal energy as we are, it did not spring from the darkness with the need to make everything balanced as we did. It is therefore, by nature flawed and inferior. It needs to know it's place."

"Elohim, brother. I mean no disrespect but aren't we defying that need to create balance by creating her to begin with?" Lucifer countered. I think all of us winced when he said that. You couldn't argue the logic but Elohim didn't like to be wrong. His eyes narrowed. Lucifer felt the need to continue, he always was overbold. "After all, we are essentially creating her to do part of our mission which means she has to be more intelligent and creative than anything else we have made. This automatically makes her out of balance."

"Must you always try to humiliate me?" Elohim snapped.

"Nothing could be further from my mind." Lucifer's continued, his tone silken and soft. "I just want this creation to be successful. We all know how hard you work to keep everything running smoothly throughout the universe. The others and myself, we are merely helpers. Truly you are the one who bears the most responsibility since you must make the final choice of which creations to bring to life. If you truly feel she should be hobbled and made less than what she could be I understand. It just seems a waste to make your greatest creation a shadow of her true potential."

Of all of us, Lucifer had always known how to appease Elohim's ruffled feathers. He had always been able to see into what truly motivated others. It had seemed to us that Lucifer could never truly push Elohim into anger. I guess everyone has their breaking point. Elohim mumbled and grumbled, which usually meant that he was once again going to give in.

"You may have a point. This creation will have a larger task than the others, it should have more resources available to it to do that. What do the rest of you think?" That was the other thing that happened constantly, the two of them would come to a grudging agreement and then ask our opinion on things. No matter which way you went you risked upsetting one or the other. We all stood there for a minute, trying to gauge our responses correctly. Slowly all the others started looking at me. I have no idea how I had become the speaker for the group. I remember thinking I was going to have some sharp words with my brothers after I talked us out of this awkward situation.

"Well, it seems to me that you are the ones who have put all the time and effort into this creation with a certain thing in mind." I aimed for a neutral position. "I don't think any of us really have a right to tell you what to do with it. The final decision, as always, rests with you Elohim." As I finished speaking I caught a quick glare from Lucifer. I decided to amend my statement. "You both raise a valid point though, since we are expecting much more from it, it should be given more knowledge and freedom." His glare shifted into a more approving look. The others just nodded in agreement, such great helps they were. Elohim and Lucifer stared at each other, neither one truly willing to give an inch.

Lucifer finally offered a bit of a compromise."She's not going to be immortal like us. We can make her mate more controlled if she seems too independent and reckless. Then work on how to control their offspring if we allow them that. She is only one creation. How much damage can she truly do?"

If we had known then what was going to happen I think all of us would have just torn her lifeless body apart and never let either Lucifer or Elohim attempt that idea ever again. That's the one thing I have never understood about the various beliefs that have grown up around us. How could any of you truly believe there was an actual plan in all of this? If Elohim was truly omniscient

8

and knew the future, why would he not have stopped all of it before it happened? Trust me, not a one of us had any idea of what was going to result from this decision to create a more complex being.

Elohim let his eyes drop from Lucifer's, we all knew what that meant. "Perhaps I am being overcautious with this creation. It is truly just one being. Let us see what it can do before we decide to limit it. If nothing else I can just not make it a mate and let it die out in the normal course of life. It is time to see what we have truly wrought my brother." Elohim extended his hands over her chest and face. "Breathe my creation, witness the world around you. Open your eyes and live."

 We felt the vibration of his words echo in and around us, the world trembled for an instant, then she took a shuddering breath. She opened her eyes, the first thing she saw was Lucifer as he had leaned over her as soon as Elohim finished speaking.

"Oh, she's truly a masterpiece!" Lucifer was almost breathless with excitement.

She looked from side to side, shifted her arms and legs, trying to figure out how her body worked. Within seconds she was sitting up. It seemed she picked things up quickly. I will always remember how she locked eyes with each one of us in turn, you could see her mind already starting to work. She tilted her head to one side and slowly bent one of her legs in preparation to stand, then she bent the other one, leaned forward and stood upright.

"Marvelous!" he cried, "Look at her, she's already learning how to move! The design truly works!"

Perhaps I should explain Lucifer's giddiness. Admittedly there were animals we had already created that walked on two legs but if you look at how they are engineered it is quite a bit different than how humans move about. Many of them still lean forward to balance correctly. She was the first truly upright, bipedal creature with proportional, useful arms we had created. We were all excited with the improvements but Lucifer's enthusiasm for his creation went far beyond all of ours, even Elohim's,

"Yes, it is wondrous Lucifer." Elohim's tone did not match his words. "Try not to get too excited about it. Of course it figured out the movement. We designed it to move that way."

She took a few shaky steps, Lucifer placed a steadying hand on her arm. "Careful child." He couldn't seem to take his eyes off of her. Elohim's face darkened, concern and disapproval simmered in his eyes.

She looked at Lucifer's hand on her arm, her hand slowly came up and covered his, an inquisitive look graced her features. He opened his hand under hers. She copied the movement. Their fingers opened and closed on top of each other, her hand clasping his. He slowly turned his hand over so their palms were touching and softly gripped her hand. "This is how you use them. Look." Lucifer guided her over to a tree that had some low hanging fruit on it, he reached up and pulled some off the branch, she quickly copied him. "Well done! Watch, this is the important part for you." He brought the fruit up to his mouth and took a bite and she copied him. A smile crossed her face as she experienced all the various tastes. It appeared she was born hungry since she devoured that first fruit in record time.

As she reached up to grab another one she paused to look at Lucifer. He hadn't eaten his since we don't get hungry. If we eat something it's because we are in the mood to taste something, not because we need it. She didn't know that though, a confused look crossed her face. Taking hold of Lucifer's fruit bearing hand with her empty one she pushed it towards his face. He took another bite, she smiled and resumed acquiring her second fruit. I will

10

never forget the look on his face when she did that simple act. Ultimate love, that was what softened his features and filled his face with joy. Her simple act of concern had captured the heart of a divine being.

"Amazing!" Uriel's quiet voice came from behind me. "I think they actually accomplished it. She understands the concept of sharing and compassion already."

"Yes, well we shall see how long that lasts." Elohim's voice was harsh. "Lucifer, you should not dote upon her so. Let her figure things out on her own, the other creations did."

"I shall do as I wish brother." His eyes locked with Elohim's. "I helped create her, I shall guide her and teach her the importance of harmony and balance in this world. We can't expect her to figure out all that on her own."

We all exchanged worried glances. Lucifer and Elohim eyed each other as the tension between them grew.

Michael attempted to calm the situation. "This is not the only world in our care Lucifer. You cannot spend all your time here. I think that is what Elohim is trying to say."

"I know my responsibilities and I am perfectly capable of teaching her and upholding them." Lucifer's arm curled around her shoulders as if to protect her from Elohim and us. "I appreciate the unneeded concern. Now if you'll excuse us, there is a great deal to cover." The two of them walked away, his hand placed protectively on the small of her back.

"Brothers," Seraqual said softly. "Lucifer will tire of her, as he always does with any new exciting creation he makes. Let him teach her, I don't find this creation all that pleasing. No offense Elohim, but she will not keep the balance, I am sure of it. We should not make her a mate anytime soon."

"We may not need to make her a mate." Raguel muttered.

Elohim spun around to face him, rage in his eyes. Raguel had never known when to keep his mouth shut. "How dare you suggest such an abomination? She's made from dirt and ash, he from the universe itself. There can never be a mating between them!"

"Brother," Raguel tended to not think about how his words affected others, "she may not come from the divine energy itself but there is something about her. You don't think Lucifer created her using the same process as the bugs, plants and animals we've made. You both were much more ambitious than that with her, Lucifer is not one to do something half way. We all sensed it when she awoke. She's different."

Elohim's fists clenched and he stormed away from us. I turned to Raguel, "Well done Raguel, well done. Are you trying to get him even angrier?"

"Elohim is always angry about something. I just speak the truth."

"It's not what you speak, it's when and how you choose to speak it. All of that could have waited until we truly see what this new creation does." I pointed out.

"Lucifer is teaching her." Michael sat down on the ground, sadness in his eyes. "What do you think she will do? As much as I love him, he's prideful and always has been."

"Oh and Elohim is better?" Raguel asked. "Really Michael, he's just as bad. Lucifer has always done his part in creating worlds. Sure he's arrogant about certain things but he has a right, he does make truly beautiful things. You can't deny that. Elohim's only real strength is bringing things to life. Admittedly, it's an important strength but he has no real skill at design like Lucifer does. He's always been jealous of Lucifer's skill. Remember, this was Elohim's idea originally. If things go badly don't hold just Lucifer to blame. Elohim wanted a helper, Lucifer just went along with the challenge. We don't need a helper and we all know that. I think Elohim was looking for something he could control, something that would be loyal to him. I don't know why."

"Brothers," Uriel interjected. "We are condemning them before they actually do anything worthy of such thoughts. The two of them have always been able to come to terms with each other. I agree with Seraquel. Lucifer will soon tire of this new creation. He and Elohim will resolve their differences as they always have. We have other things to attend to that are more important than all this ill-guided chatter."

Uriel tended to serve as our scheduler. I never knew how he managed to keep track of everything we were working on and what stage it was at. We had learned over the years that if he said it was time to be at a certain place to head there as fast as possible. I had always liked him because he always managed to look at everything in a rational, calm way. He had his mission and that was all that mattered to him. The fact that he was the only one of my brothers that I was taller than might have influenced my opinion on him as well. None of us ever doubted his strength or power though. His aura was shimmering green, like a moving forest, his dark brown skin and hair complemented it well. All those dark colors made his pale blue eyes stand out that much more in his face.

"Yes, Uriel you are right as always." Raphael agreed. "This is all fascinating to ponder but a bit hasty. We should be about our other tasks, worlds await us."

"Perhaps one of us should stay here, keep an eye on the two of

13

them." Gabriel spoke. He had been abnormally quiet on the topic of Lillith's creation the whole time Lucifer and Elohim had been working on her. He usually shared some sort of opinion on things but this time he seemed almost afraid to say anything at all. "I dislike what I have seen and am seeing from both of them regarding this new creation."

"Well Uriel," I asked. "Who can be spared from the other tasks at this time?"

"Your tasks are proceeding well Remiel so you could stay as could Gabriel."

"I can stay then I guess if you don't want to Gabriel." I offered.

"I'll stay as well," he replied. "I could use the break and I am curious to see how she progresses under Lucifer's tutelage. Besides, you being stuck here alone with the two of them might drive you mad." A small grin crossed his face.

"I appreciate that, you're probably right. I guess that's it then. Just check in on us when you can brothers." I hadn't really wanted to stay but I agreed with Gabriel, something was different between them this time and someone would be needed to sort things out.

"I'll inform you when your tasks need attention brothers. Until then." Uriel shimmered and disappeared, the others did as well, leaving Gabriel and myself alone. I watched as his blue aura stirred restlessly.

"Gabriel? Talk, you've been too quiet about this. What's troubling you?" Cloudy grey eyes briefly locked with mine, then he looked away and started to pace back and forth.

"I have had misgivings about this latest creation. There is no real purpose for it, I have not felt the connection with this creation as

14

with the others. I don't think any of us have."

The connection that he spoke of is hard to describe. Normally when we would create something we would get a message or a hunch from the universe. Sometimes it was an image of what the new creation was to look like or what niche in the balance it was to fill. The energy of the universe required something to maintain the balance and that is how it told us what to make. As far as I knew, none of us had received any messages about creating Lillith. The way Lucifer and Elohim had spoken of her when they were creating her, it was pretty obvious to us that they were doing this on their own. They had created her with no real guidance or idea of how to start. We would get at least an idea of how to start if there was something we were required to make.

"I know, I haven't either," I said. "You have to admit though that this isn't the first time we've changed things without guidance."

"That was changing things that already existed which is entirely different," he pointed out, "We changed them to adjust to the balance. All things grow and change, even the balance. That ridiculous platypus or the other oddities we created by accident or small whim, they were not nearly as powerful or disruptive as this creation is. However odd they were, they still filled a need and were in balance. They do not compare to this."

He had a point. "True, but I am not sure about what to do now. The two of them are incredibly stubborn. They can't destroy her, that is forbidden even to Elohim. Perhaps all we can do is minimize the disruption to the balance if needed. Don't let her reproduce."

Gabriel stopped his pacing and looked at me, sadness and apprehension written on his features."We all saw his face Remiel. Lucifer views her as something more. Denying it won't change that. We are all charged with keeping the balance, especially

15

Elohim. Lucifer caring for a creation like this, it is not in balance. I feel it already, there is a storm gathering. Michael feels it too. We have to convince Lucifer of this."

"Why are we focusing on Lucifer? Elohim is as much at fault for bringing her to life as Lucifer is." It bothered me that a few of my brothers seemed eager to single out Lucifer for some sort of retribution.

"Elohim doesn't get attached. He would have created her and left her to her own devices," Gabriel said.

"Are we all so sure that Elohim is angry about the balance of the universe and not about Lucifer wanting to treat her the way that perhaps she should be?" I countered, "Elohim doesn't like competition of any kind for anything, especially what he feels is his due. It was fairly obvious that he wanted to create some sort of servant, not an equal. I don't understand why he gave in to Lucifer on that point."

"Yes you do. Elohim never denies the Morningstar anything. In the end Lucifer always gets his way. We all know who the most powerful of us is and it is not Elohim. Lucifer's power of persuasion controls the giver of life. Elohim has always overly admired and indulged our brother. That is why we are all focusing on Lucifer. Elohim is already angered and he never thinks when he is angry. If he were to talk to Lucifer all that would occur would be an argument and things would escalate. We must stop Lucifer from becoming more attached to this creation before it is too late." His usually mobile features stilled, apprehension had quickly changed into resolve.

Have you ever had a moment in your life where you know, just know there is precipice looming in front of you? You don't understand why your heart races and your palms sweat when considering a small conversation or meeting. Phrases such as "It's just temporary" or "Nothing is written in stone" or "I have a backup plan" or "He'll listen, of course he will" run through your mind in a futile attempt to calm yourself down. Deep down, in your heart of hearts, you hear that voice telling you that those things are all lies, that the situation has already escalated, the course irreversible. Then the dreaded question of "How did I get here?" slams into your mind. Gabriel's gentle nature was slowly being eroded, the sadness and anger that Michael expressed was completely unexpected, both of them were already wondering how we had gotten to this moment. I was unsure as to what the moment held for the future but it was fairly obvious that sides were already being chosen. I paused, I had to choose my next words with care.

"We are equals Gabriel. We are brothers, family. We all bear the responsibility for our choices and creations, we cannot blame one of us above the others. They asked for our input, however ill-timed and manipulative the question was. None of you spoke up against it, you all turned to me. If you had had misgivings earlier, it rested upon you or Michael to raise them. I will talk to Lucifer but I will not blame him more than Elohim or any of the rest of us if things fall out of balance."

Gabriel turned away from me, my heart dropped into that precipice I had sensed. "Perhaps you are right and the fault of this is on all of us. I will find Elohim and see if I can calm him. I wish you luck with Lucifer." He took a step away from me and vanished.

A sense of foreboding seemed to slowly fill the idyllic meadow I stood in, the shadows drew closer and the temperature cooled. For the entirety of my memories I had always felt the sense of my brothers in my mind, we were connected, all beings of the same energy. Yet as I stood there, trying to come up with the best way to discuss things with Lucifer a new sensation slowly filled me. I felt alone. I had never felt alone before. Sides were indeed being

17

drawn. It seemed that the words I had just barely finished speaking had somehow damaged the bonds my brothers and I had shared for eternity. How had we gotten here?

CHAPTER 2

I tracked Lucifer and Lillith down, they were sitting by a small stream and Lucifer was teaching her the names of things and how to speak. Part of me wanted to hang back in the shadows and watch but that just felt wrong, as if I was spying on my brother, who, as far as I could see hadn't really done anything wrong. I walked out from the trees and headed towards them.

"May I join you? Turns out I don't have much going on elsewhere at the moment."

Lucifer turned around and smiled. He appeared to have lost his earlier anger, or maybe that was aimed more at Elohim than the rest of us. "Of course brother, Lillith should get to know all of you."

He had given her a name, that was not good. "Lillith? Is that the name of her species?" I was hoping I had misunderstood him.

"No, that's her name. I haven't come up with a name for her kind yet but I thought the name was beautiful, like she is." He beamed at me, then looked back at her. "Lillith, this is Remiel. He is one of my brothers."

Lillith's face turned towards me, once again I was struck by her beauty and her lack of fear when she looked at me. She had certainly been gifted with Lucifer's confidence.

"Re..mi...el," she spoke slowly, sounding out the syllables.

"Perfect! Try it again!" Lucifer encouraged her.

"Remiel." It came much faster this time, she smiled at me.

"Hello Lillith. Well done. What have you learned so far?" I may as well play along to see what I could learn.

She pointed at the water, "That's a stream, this tree is an aspen, that is dirt, there are fish in the water but I don't know what they look like. Lucifer says he will get me a fish later. Oh and up above us is sky and beyond that is the universe which I can't see." A bird flew by "That's a bird." She certainly was a fast learner.

"Have you told her what her task is?" I asked Lucifer.

"In time I will. I think that's a bit complicated for her to understand just yet."

"Do you even know what her task is?"

Lucifer's face darkened. He stood up. "Lillith, stay here a minute, my brother and I need to talk."

"I will do as you say." Lillith returned to her contemplation of the lake, probably waiting for a fish to jump out of the water. Lucifer walked away from her and beckoned me to follow.

"Is there a particular reason all of you are against me?" He snarled, his aura started flashing and flickering around him.

"I'm not for or against anyone." I reassured him. "None of us felt that the universe was calling for this being to be created so what is her role in the balance? That is what is the most important thing here, maintaining the balance."

"Elohim wanted to create her, I merely helped," he snapped out "I saw it as a challenge. If you have a question as to the balance of the universe take it up with him. He would have created her and left her alone with no guidance. He's mad at me for showing her attention. He wanted some sort of slave or worshiper which is most certainly not within the balance. I am trying to give her a chance to be something more."

The whole concept of a worshiper confused me at the time. We didn't require a creation to pray to us, we draw our power from the universe.

"A worshiper, what's that?" I asked

"He wants a creation that sees him as all powerful. Our brother has become even more wrapped up in his hubris than usual. Honestly Remiel, I don't know what her task is. When Elohim came to me with the idea I thought it would be an interesting task, at least from a design perspective. Something that walks like we do, that can talk and think like we do. My mind was filled with possibilities and concepts and that was all I thought about to begin with. The longer we worked on it the more apparent it became to me that Elohim wanted something that would rule this planet and carry out his orders. What those orders would be I have no idea. It's not like we get involved in day to day dealings on these worlds we build. Then he started muttering on about experimenting with her kind and seeing what they could build and do and to have a place where he could come and people would see his true worth. I think something is wrong with him." He paused.

"If you felt something was wrong with this whole idea or wrong with him why didn't you stop him and bring it to our attention?" It seemed to me that no one had bothered to try to stop Elohim, including me. We had gotten so used to deferring to him on certain things that we just took this odd task in stride, besides, no one liked dealing with his temper when he was angry.

"I tried once or twice, he exploded into a rage and threatened to finish her without my help. By then I knew that if that happened she would be a disastrous creation and he would abuse her in some way. I couldn't let that happen. I didn't bring it to the rest of you because of how I knew you all would react. Michael would back Elohim, Uriel would stay neutral, Gabriel would want to not bring her to life, Raguel and Seraqual wouldn't care, Raphael would urge caution and you'd try to find a reasonable solution. Nothing would be resolved in the end and Elohim would bring her to life anyway out of spite. So I decided to help and make her something truly special....," His voice grew quiet, he was leaving something out.

"What did you do?" I remembered Raguel stating something was different about her, I hadn't noticed it at first but when she locked eyes with me and tried to say my name I had felt it then.

He looked at me, defiance in his gaze. He was challenging me to condemn him for what he was about to tell me. "I gifted her with some of my energy, some of the universal spark. I didn't think I could but I figured out a way to do it."

"You what! How? Why? Lucifer, this is wrong and you know it! Wait, if you did that before Elohim brought her to life then what was with the whole debate earlier? You didn't tell him did you." I was stunned. If I was right Lucifer had manipulated the whole conversation that morning to get Elohim to allow him to do what he had already done. Honestly, it still stuns me to this day. That was the first time I truly realized how truly devious Lucifer could be.

"Of course not! Do you take me for a fool? Elohim would never approve. That's one reason he was so upset when she woke up, he sensed it. By then he couldn't do anything about it. The whole scene this morning was an act on my part, I knew he would want to constrain her so I had to get him to say yes. He would never admit he made a mistake or back down from a position he had already taken. He's so predictable.

Remiel, listen to me please. Everything we make has a right to live its life without belonging to something or someone else. Creation should not worship at the feet of its creator, life is about freedom, not obeisance. The animals, plants and insects, they have roles to play true, and are in some ways constrained by their form but they are still free to live their own life. There is no being telling them what to do and how to do it. Elohim wanted to make something that would not be free, that would be bound to listen to him. That goes completely against the balance of the universe. By giving her some of my energy, some of my spark I tried to put her back in balance. If I had not helped and Elohim had created something that was bound to him things would be worse."

I didn't know what to say. The whole idea that Lucifer had completely manipulated all of us was so foreign at the time. Admittedly he had always worked around Elohim before but this was on a much deeper level than ever before. He had not just twisted Elohim to get what he thought was right, but all of us. What was even more upsetting was that he thought he knew what all of us would say and chose to dismiss us outright in favor of his own opinion on things.

"So you disregarded all of us in this. If Elohim's judgment is truly clouded for whatever reason we all need to be aware of it. You speak of Elohim's hubris but what of your own? Be honest Lucifer, don't try to smooth things over with me like you do with Elohim." Now that I was aware of how his mind was working when it came to Lillith I wasn't sure if I could believe anything he said from that point on. I hoped that since I was the weakest of us he would see little reason to try to manipulate me.

He looked away from me and stared at Lillith who was innocently playing with a rock. She was manipulating it in her hands completely fascinated by the textures she felt. Lucifer's face held such love and concern for her, he truly felt like he needed to teach her and protect her from Elohim. I began to understand the warnings of my brothers.

"She's a mere child," his voice was soft and gentle but filled with determination. Slowly his aura of power grew brighter and brighter, I almost had to look away from him it had grown so strong. "She should never be forced to feel something that is not real. We would not do that to each other. Why should we do that to our creations? Perhaps I was wrong in not speaking to you and the others about it but I did what I thought was right."

I had to speak up about what the others were feeling, Lucifer had to know what his actions could cause. "I understand and agree with you on that point but there's something I think you overlooked in your calculations about our brothers." His eyes focused on mine. "Some of them see this attachment as a danger, they are blaming you because we all know you always persuade Elohim. I don't know what is going on but sides are being chosen. They are concerned that this will cause a permanent rift between you and Elohim. Michael feels that you are prideful, Raguel has already pointed out you have stronger feelings for her than you should, Gabriel thinks that you will become so focused on her that you will ignore your other tasks. If you truly added this spark of you to her without Elohim's approval he will not easily forgive that insult. Gabriel spoke of a storm gathering, he and Michael are afraid of some sort of conflict between the two of you. Please, please listen to me. I agree with your points I just think you need to not be so protective of her. Don't compound the insult." Looking back I should have never said that last sentence. Lucifer had seemed to be willing to listen to me until I spoke those last words. I had forgotten about his arrogance in my concern for the situation.

"Why is everyone always trying to appease Elohim?" Darkness and anger came out with those words. "He does nothing but complain and throw tantrums to get his way. I am tired of it. I will summon Uriel and have him call everyone back, I will explain the situation as it happened. However they choose to view me at that point is up to them. Now, leave me. Go report back to Gabriel, I know he's not far away." Lucifer returned to Lillith's side, leaving me speechless. I knew that Gabriel would have even less success in getting Elohim to calm down, especially if Lucifer had indeed not informed him about giving Lillith some of his energy and divine spark. I wanted very badly to get all my brothers together and talk this out but I could already see that we were far past any chance of that.

I could have easily sent myself to exactly where Gabriel was, teleporting as it came to be called. Back then we always knew where everyone was, part of being connected to the universe on an energetic level. I needed time to think, so I chose to walk instead. My mind was spinning, Elohim had his issues but I found it hard to believe that he wanted to make some sort of slave race. For time eternal it had just been my brothers and I and the things we had created. These concepts that Lucifer was bringing up had were so completely alien I had absolutely no reference to understand them at all. What would possess Elohim to even ponder this much less go forward with the creation of Lillith? I hoped that by the time I arrived Gabriel would have him calmed down enough to be rational.

"Don't you see?" I heard Elohim's fierce voice and my hope died. As I walked through a shady grove of trees I could see their auras well before I saw them. It was hard to miss the auras, my brothers had grown so agitated that sparks of light were actually reaching higher than the tree line. It appeared that once again I had to play peace bringer.

"Gabriel, Elohim, you're going to destroy this forest if you don't calm down."

"Remiel! Who asked you here anyway?" That would be Elohim. Gabriel turned to face me, a mix of hopelessness and frustration in his face.

"I didn't think I needed permission to stay on this world." My voice was a tad sharp.

"Did you get answers?" Gabriel asked. I chose to remain silent and just shrugged. I doubted mentioning Lucifer would help the situation.

Elohim glared at me. "Yes, pray tell. How is the selfish brother doing? Is he pleased with what he stole from me?" Apparently I didn't need to mention him.

"Can we all try to calm down please? I want to know what is going on with you Elohim. Can you please explain why you and Lucifer wanted to create her?" I almost said Lillith but caught myself at the last minute. If they knew he had given her a name things would be much worse.

"Fine!"

I'll state now that I was in no way prepared for the explanation Elohim was about to give me. I still shudder when I think of it. It wasn't just what he said but the look on his face. There was madness there and a twisted arrogance I had never seen before. Perhaps we had all come to accept his arrogance but never realized how much it was driving his decisions. As he spoke his aura grew darker, flickers of amber light flashed about the clearing we were standing in. I think that was the first time in my long life I had ever felt fear.

"Let me ask both of you this. What is it that we do? Who are we really?"

I looked at Elohim, confused as to why he was asking such questions. "We create life and maintain the balance of things. We are the tools of the universe itself," I answered.

"That's it? That's the entirety of what you think we are Remiel? How simple of you. We have spent eternity, or perhaps even longer than that creating plants and animals, insects, air and water. To what greater purpose? These things that we create, they do not recognize us as their creators. They do not appreciate what it is we do or have done for them? We are invisible to them, ever present but never truly observed or appreciated. Tell me. Are you truly satisfied with creating yet another plant? Either of you?" Elohim stared at Gabriel and myself in turn. There was an air of superiority and condescension about him, one side of his mouth was curled up in an impatient smirk as if we were not worthy of his time or an explanation.

"What is the point to it? Are we to just go on forever, endlessly creating mindless things that have no respect for us and no concept of how truly fortunate they are to simply exist? No! We deserve better. Have you never been frustrated when you walked by a beast that we just brought to life and it neither recognizes you nor expresses any gratitude to you for bringing it to life? All these things we have done, it's not the universe that did it. We did, you, our brothers and I. We chose what to make, when to make it, how to make it and what it would do."

"But Elohim, we are from the universe, we receive instructions from it. That is how we know what to do." Gabriel had stepped away from Elohim and addressed him in soft, soothing tones. He clearly did not want to push Elohim even further.

"Gabriel, dearest brother. Did it never occur to you that maybe those "messages" are just our own thoughts? Come now, you don't think that after all this time we don't have our own ideas and intuition on how to create worlds. Do either of you truly remember our beginning? How we came to be?"

27

I could see Gabriel starting to become confused. Truly I could not answer Elohim's question. I just remembered always existing and knowing what it was that I had to do.

"We've always just existed, you know that as well as I do." I put much more confidence in my voice than I felt. Gabriel's evident and increasing confusion was disconcerting and I was desperately trying to find some way to refute Elohim's questions. We had never pondered the beginning, it had never seemed important, at least not to me. I was actually content creating things and watching life grow, change and evolve. Philosophy was too abstract for my tastes. Elohim threw his arms up in disgust, obviously not happy with my answer.

"This is why I never speak of these things to you. You are content. You don't think beyond your current assignment. It's pointless." He made as if to turn away.

Gabriel reached out and grabbed Elohim's arm. "No, you're not walking away from this. Explain her, explain this obsession. You may not like our way of thinking but we deserve an answer."

Elohim's eyes dropped to Gabriel's hand. "Remove your hand brother, I'll not be ordered about by you."

Gabriel didn't remove his hand, his eyes narrowed and he stepped further into Elohim's space. Their auras started to spark and merge as they came into such close contact with one another. For the first time ever I saw smoke rise from my brother's bodies.

"Enough!" I put my hand on Gabriel's shoulder. "There is no need for this, whatever this is. Just explain yourself, Elohim, please." Elohim jerked his arm away from Gabriel and turned to face me and only me.

"It's simple Remiel. We, the nine of us, we are the universe. There is no other thing that controls us. You just refuse to recognize it. I bring things to life, not you, not Lucifer, not Michael or anyone else. I decide what to bring to life, I always have. I am not guided by anyone or anything. I have tired of my creations being mindless and pointless. She was to be the first of a whole series of creations that would be aware of who we are, who I am."

"To what purpose," I interrupted.

I watched as his eyes narrowed and a sneer slowly spread across his mouth. Slowly he leaned towards me, looking into my eyes the whole time as if he felt the need to intimidate me.

"To show me the respect I deserve for creating them. Lucifer ruined her but now that I know how to make them, I will make more. I no longer need assistance from him or any of you."

Elohim shoved me away. Stunned, I fell back and landed heavily on the ground. I had never been shoved before in my life.

He glared a challenge at Gabriel who stood motionless and afraid. "That's the proper decision Gabriel, don't interfere with me. It's about time all of you realized that without me, you are meaningless. Lucifer designs beautiful things, but only I can truly create life. He'll soon realize that for all his skill, he has no power, he will always have to come to me in the end." Elohim turned away from us and disappeared.

CHAPTER 3

Gabriel and I were too astonished to move.

"What just happened?" Poor Gabriel, he hadn't had any prior warning about Elohim's madness. I may not have wholly believed Lucifer but at least I had had a few minutes to start getting used to the idea.

"Lucifer spoke of this. I didn't want to accept what he told me as truth but it appears he wasn't exaggerating. If anything, he underestimated how much Elohim has changed." I slowly stood back up at the same time Gabriel sank to the ground. My brother was shaking.

"Remiel, what is all this? What does it mean? How do we stop them?"

"I don't know if we can or what it means. We need to call all of our brothers together. Lucifer said he'd be willing to tell everyone his side."

Gabriel's head was bowed, he dug his fingers into the ground.

"We should have stopped him before it got this far, Michael and I. We had a chance, we thought ourselves too busy to get involved."

"What do you mean?"

"Elohim came to us, to discuss his plans for this new creation. He wanted our help at first, not Lucifer's. The Morningstar may be Elohim's favorite among us but he knows how independent Lucifer can be. Elohim said that he wanted to design a creation based off of the two of us because we have always been the most faithful to him. Michael and I thought the whole idea nonsense and told him so, then we left to take care of other assignments. I guess he went to Lucifer after that. If only we had agreed to help him maybe we could have built in a flaw that would have made it fail and he would have given up. Once Lucifer starts working on a challenge he keeps at it until what he is creating is perfect. He would not have purposely made a creation fail. His solution to the problem has made it much worse. In making her a truly independent and intelligent creature he has pushed Elohim even further. Now he won't stop until he gets exactly what he wants."

"Is that why you and Michael both referred to some sort of storm coming? You already knew what his plans were. You knew what he was working on and it never dawned on either of you to mention something was a bit off."

I couldn't believe what I was hearing. I remember I had a brief conversation with Michael and Elohim about this new creation but at the time I was deep into figuring out how to create mammals that lived underwater and hadn't really paid too much attention.

His eyes flashed with anger. "Understand we weren't completely aware of the extent of his design. He never mentioned this whole concept of wanting creations to fawn over him. You are not completely blameless here. Elohim spoke with all of us at one point or another. If anyone is truly to blame it is Lucifer. He should have informed us as soon as he realized Elohim's true intentions."

There it was again, Lucifer as the problem. The constant refrain of "Blame Lucifer" was starting to anger me. There was a crackling sound, the world became tinted with a lavender haze and the air heated up around me. Gabriel's eyes began to widen and he slowly backed away. I didn't understand at first, then realized that my anger was causing my aura to flare. As far as I can remember that was the first time I had truly experienced anger, I wish I could say it was the last. It was a struggle getting these new emotions under control and I'll admit I took a few steps towards Gabriel before I could stop myself.

Closing my eyes I turned away from him and slowly calmed myself. "My apologies brother. There is no point blaming each other or Lucifer. The true problem is Elohim, he will not stop until his vision is realized. That is what we need to focus on for now. Please summon Uriel, Michael and Raguel. I will call for Seraqual, Raphael and Lucifer. We must decide together what our next steps should be."

"Shouldn't we call for Elohim as well?" Gabriel asked.

"Not yet." Yet another decision I came to regret later. "It will only result in another argument between he and Lucifer and nothing will be accomplished. One thing at a time. Let's see what our brothers have to say about this before we confront Elohim again."

Gabriel nodded, closed his eyes and started to summon our brothers. We had to be quiet about it as it was entirely possible that Elohim would feel the energy we sent out to summon the others. I had a feeling that in his arrogance he would just ignore it. I summoned Lucifer and the others and within a few minutes they all appeared. Lucifer had brought Lillith, apparently he wasn't too keen on leaving her unattended. I cringed when I saw her, her presence would only add additional difficulties but apparently he had thought ahead. He lightly touched her forehead and she fell asleep, that took me by surprise. I wasn't aware that we had the ability to do that.

"How did you do that?" I asked.

"I'm not sure, I just told her to sleep and she did."

Between the new feelings of anger, the experience of Elohim shoving me, Lucifer's revelations about Elohim, what he gifted Lillith with and this new use of our powers I had reached a breaking point.

"Perhaps you should share these new developments with all of us for once instead of assuming we aren't worth your time." I snapped, the world was once again shaded in lavender overtones.

"Remiel? What are you doing?" Uriel's soft voice came from behind me. I turned and saw the confusion and concern on my brother's faces.

"Brothers, Elohim has greatly overstepped his bounds. This creation of his was not about a design challenge or creating a helpmate, it was about making something to worship him. It is hard to explain. I have spoken to both Elohim and Lucifer about this, Gabriel spoke with Elohim as well. We are all at fault for not noticing these things sooner however Elohim is the true concern, not what we did or did not choose to do with whatever knowledge we had at the time." That was my attempt at directing their focus away from Lucifer and to Elohim. "Lucifer, as you were the one most directly involved I think you should tell us everything that happened." I hoped that he would make sure to include what he gifted Lillith with. I didn't want to have to bring it up myself. He looked at me, his eyes narrowed a bit but he gave me a slight nod. It seemed he understood that if he wanted me as an ally he would have to include his earlier deception of us along with his deception of Elohim.

He put on his most charming expression, "Sit brothers, this will take some time." Raphael and Michael gave him an uneasy look, Seraqual, Raguel and Uriel seemed curious but showed no signs of concern. How I wished I could have joined them in their ignorance. We sat down on the ground in a rough circle. A few sparrows landed in the center of the circle and pecked at the ground looking for seeds. Raguel created a handful of seeds on the spot and sprinkled them on the ground in front of him. The birds hopped over and he lightly rubbed their heads as they ate. He had always been fond of any creature that could fly. Lucifer began to speak.

"When Elohim came to me with the idea of this new creation I will admit that I was immediately intrigued by the concept. As you all know I always seek out the most complicated things to design. Perhaps my desire to create something wholly new and different overruled any misgivings I may have felt about his goals."

"In the beginning it seemed like a harmless way to pass the time, Elohim and I exchanged ideas and spent many hours thoroughly engulfed in the project. You do have to admit brothers that we have all done the same over the eons, become utterly enthralled by a new idea, a new creature. It consumes you, you think of little else, even to the point of boring the rest of us."

Before that morning I would have been nodding along with Lucifer, just as most of my brothers were. Now that I knew how devious and silken tongued he could be I kept my mind much more alert to what he was really doing, not merely what he was saying. This was shaping up to be another masterful performance on his part and I found myself hoping he could truly make the others realize what our true concern should be.

"As time went on Elohim started to speak of confusing, complicated things. He seemed to be more and more concerned that our creations didn't truly understand how blessed they were that they had been made. To be honest brothers, I wasn't really able to comprehend the complexity of what he was saying. I, like all of you, have always been quite content with what our roles in the universe are. We are tools of the will of the universe, we are truly fortunate to be part of the forces of creation. I expressed this to him and it only seemed to agitate him more; he said I was too simple and content, that I should look around myself and see what we truly are." He paused and looked at each of us in turn.

As if on cue Seraqual asked the question, giving Lucifer the perfect opening. "What did he say we are?"

"At first I was too nervous to ask him what he meant. I much preferred discussing design than philosophy. However the closer and closer to completing the design we came, the more and more unstable he seemed to be. He started speaking of wanting a creation that would appreciate him and us, that would be thankful, that would recognize that we were responsible for it's existence." Lucifer stood up and started pacing, as if becoming agitated over the memories of the conversations he had had with Elohim. "I was astonished brothers. After all, that is not our purpose." He closed his eyes and wrapped his arms around himself.

I was still the only one that knew to what extent Lucifer could act and it took all I had to keep myself from educating my brothers that he was not as upset as he appeared. My brothers were all leaning towards him, hanging on his every word and gesture.

Michael was even more solemn than usual."Wait, he wanted to create something that would recognize us. I don't understand the purpose behind that." He exchanged a glance with Gabriel and I saw a hint of guilt in that glance. It seemed that Michael's thoughts were traveling the same path that Gabriel's had when we had spoken earlier.

Lucifer opened his eyes, resignation and fear colored his face. As I looked into his eyes I came to realize that what he showed to us at that moment was indeed honest. The manipulator disappearing for a brief moment. "He thinks our creations should feel a debt of eternal gratitude to us. It seems he has forgotten that we too come from something greater than ourselves."

35

Uriel was the first to really react to what Lucifer had said. "Let me make sure I am clear on this," he said. He carefully placed his elbows on his crossed knees and and rested his chin on his hands. He seemed calm, at least until you looked into his pale blue eyes, they were anything but calm. "Elohim is placing himself above the universe, us and the balance that we are supposed to uphold?"

"It appears that way," Lucifer replied. Uriel looked at me, seeking some sort of verification.

"What Lucifer says is true. Elohim expressed the same things to Gabriel and myself. There is more but I feel Lucifer should continue. Gabriel and I will tell our sides when he is done." I didn't want any of what had happened to remain a secret.

"I am getting a bit ahead of what happened," Lucifer stated.

"Thank you for keeping me on track Remiel." It was obvious, at least to me, that gratitude was not exactly what he was feeling at that moment. "By this point she was almost done. I was torn, I wanted him to bring her to life because I wanted to see if the design worked but I felt that how he viewed her would upset the balance. I set her aside and went to speak with him. I appealed to him to further explain what he meant. He launched into quite a speech but I will sum it up for all of you. Elohim feels that there is nothing beyond or greater than us, that the direction we get from the universe is merely our own ideas based upon eons of building and populating worlds. He believes that since he is the only one of us that can grant the gift of life to the more complicated creatures that he is voice of the universe and therefore the balance."

Raphael lunged to his feet. "He what?" Emerald green flashes darted around the clearing, startling all of us.

"Why didn't you call us immediately?" Raguel asked. Lucifer

looked at me, his expression unreadable.

"What would that have accomplished?" Lucifer's haughty nature reasserted itself. "Have any of you ever been capable of swaying Elohim from a chosen path like I can? Honestly brothers, if all of you had come charging in what exactly could you have done? Would you truly understand what he was proposing before this morning when he brought her to life?"

"You think you are the only one he listens to?" Michael asked. "You, as usual think too highly of your own skills."

Lucifer walked over to Michael and crouched down in front of him. "Ah yes, loyal, steadfast Michael. Elohim told me he came to you and Gabriel first with this idea and you dismissed him. I was not the only one who knew what he planned. I don't remember either of you expressing any concern this morning or before that. Perhaps I missed a meeting?" Michael's jaw tightened as his green eyes grew hard and the two of them locked gazes briefly, Michael was the first to look away.

"No you did not. Gabriel and I did not inform anyone of Elohim's plan, it is true."

"Indeed it is. Anyone else remember a conversation with Elohim about this?" Lucifer asked, waving his arm to encompass all of us. I watched as all of my brothers slowly dropped their eyes to the ground. "So then, all of you already knew."

"Not true Lucifer," Uriel stated. "We all had brief conversations with him. You were truly the only one who knew the full extent of his plans."

"I'll grant you that Uriel, however I knew that Elohim had already spoken to all of you before and each and every one of you dismissed him. What makes you think he would then take anything any of you said with any seriousness? It was I, and only I, that had worked with him on this. I felt if any of us had a chance to stop him it would be me."

Seraqual rolled his eyes, "Well, we can all see how well that worked can't we?"

Lucifer glared at him. "Elohim is nothing if not stubborn and it appeared that he had been contemplating these things for much longer than I think any of us realize. It became apparent to me that even if I did something to make this creation fail he would just keep trying and I refuse to have anything we create be forced to feel a certain way. We were created with a purpose, I have never forgotten that and will do everything I can to protect the balance. I hoped that when this one awoke and he understood that she could be aware of us without being a slave or be turned into a being who's entire purpose was to bow to him he would accept that he can be loved without being feared. It seems that is not to be."

Gabriel finally spoke up, "Perhaps if you had not been so eager to take over instructing her and at least gave him a chance to spend time with her that would have worked. From the moment she woke up she has consumed your attention."

Lucifer's pale yellow eyes flashed and his aura smoldered, a sunset consumed by fire. "She has consumed my attention because she is under my protection. He means to reduce her to nothing, where she places him above all of us. She will not be allowed to think or feel anything unless he approves of it. I gave her a gift, she has become part of me and I will not let him have her!"

"She's part of you? Explain yourself!" Michael's voice reverberated across the meadow as he lunged to his feet, briefly towering over Lucifer. Lucifer rose to his feet and encroached into Michael's space.

Fear flowed through me as I watched the rest of my brothers stand up, green, blue, lavender, silver and gold lighting flickered through the air. Power I had never felt started pressing against me, crashing into my mind. High pitched tones filled my ears as the wind started to rush by me in ever more powerful gusts.

"I found a way to impart part of my essence into her." Lucifer's words were filled with power, power none of us had ever experienced before. "I did it without telling him. That was what all of you felt when she awoke. She carries a bit of our power in her and as such will never be compelled to bow to any of us. Say what you will, I did what I thought was best to keep her safe from him."

Michael's arms flashed out to shove Lucifer away. "You have gone too far! You deceived us all this morning didn't you? Arrogant and selfish as always. We should destroy her now."

I remember feeling both sick and oddly exhilarated. "What would that accomplish? Michael stand down!" I had never ordered any of my brothers before. "Gabriel and I spoke with Elohim. He has already stated that he will make more of these since he knows how to. Are we to become destroyers and not creators?"

"If that means restoring the balance than yes!" Michael shouted back.

"How do you propose to stop Elohim from making more?" Uriel pointed out. "We can destroy every one he makes but it will not address the true problem and that is his madness. We cannot destroy him. If we do, we cannot keep the balance at all."

"Ahh Uriel. You have always seen to the true nature of things." Elohim's voice came to us from across the meadow. We all turned to face him. He slowly walked towards us, flames from his aura deflecting any lighting from us that got too close, there was a large sense of smug self satisfaction in his tone. "I'm saddened I wasn't invited to this gathering. Perhaps it is just as well, I doubt you would have been so truthful if I had been in your presence. It's so distressing to me that not a single one of you see things like I do. Look at her." He appeared next to Lillith and crouched down next to her. "Isn't she beautiful? Yet she is only that way because Lucifer and I made her so. What is so wrong with wanting her to understand that? Her intelligence, beauty, independence and even her gift of Lucifer's energy, all of that has nothing to do with her. She should appreciate that shouldn't she? How does that disturb the balance in any way?"

He stood and walked over to Lucifer whose face had grown wary, as if he realized that he had missed some crucial point in Elohim's calculations.

"Dearest, dearest Lucifer. All that skill you have is meaningless isn't it? You could design a million of her and they would all languish, lifeless unless I chose to act. Yet none of you truly seem to acknowledge that do you? It is my choice that ultimately affects this balance you are all so concerned about. What is this balance we so strive to maintain? Will the universe implode if we create one creature that shows us the respect we deserve? I doubt it. You all seem to think I am insane or disturbed in some way. I assure you I am not. Brothers, you are the ones who fail to understand. Don't worry, I am not upset at the fact that you were here conspiring against me. I understand how the ideas I am offering are overwhelming and unsettling to you. To be honest I am even thankful that Lucifer gifted her with his energy. It was something I had never contemplated before, perhaps I will add that into the next ones I create. She will need a mate after all and they should be equals don't you think?"

My brothers were all stunned into complete and utter silence.

Elohim's whole presence and attitude were so completely different than anything we had ever seen from him. He truly thought that he was the voice of the universe and his choices were the only ones that mattered. I took a deep breath and tried to reason with him.

"Please, please don't continue with this. Your power is indeed great Elohim but we all have parts to play, we all must work together. These creations, what you wish of them, I don't understand why it is so important to you that they acknowledge us. Isn't it enough that we can look upon this world and see the fruits of our labor? Why should any of the animals that move upon this world stop and bow before us?"

Elohim simply smiled. It was an arrogant, vicious smile. "Does not the prey animal stop and quiver when it senses a predator? We have built that into them have we not? We already design weaker and stronger animals to maintain the higher balance correct?"

My stomach dropped, I glanced at Lucifer. In all the years we had existed Lucifer had never looked defeated, yet he did now. He knew where Elohim was going to go with this thought and that some of our brothers would end up agreeing with him. I had to answer the question honestly. "Yes, but this is different." Even as I said it I in found myself partially agreeing with Elohim.

"No it isn't, you just haven't accepted it. Don't worry. I'll give you all time to come around. You have to eventually, after all I am the one that controls what we do, aren't I." He gave us such a look then. It was filled with utter superiority and contempt of us. "Oh and Lucifer, make sure to inform her that she will have a mate soon. I'll inform you when he is ready." He reached out his hand and patted Lucifer on the cheek then walked to Lillith and stood over her. Lucifer's hands clenched.

"Don't worry brother, I'll let her stay as she is." Elohim said, then

41

he vanished.

Chapter 4

Silence filled the meadow, nothing moved, not even a leaf. It seemed as if time itself had simply stopped with Elohim's departure. Even to this day, I remember my brothers' faces at that exact moment. Lucifer's aura shimmering in protective rage as he hovered over Lillith. Michael staring at him, such a look Michael had. It seemed to me that armor was slowly appearing on Michael's body, golden armor that encased his heart, locking it away from Lucifer and the rest of us. Seraqual and Raquel were just utterly lost and confused, Raphael kept looking between Lucifer and Michael, indecision and regret simmering on his face. Dearest Gabriel had glistening blue tears streaming down his cheeks, of all of us Uriel seemed to be the most calm, his face was still. I could see him running calculations and possible outcomes in his mind.

"She will not be compelled to be with any mate he makes." Lucifer spoke and something in his voice compelled us to listen. The velvet tones, singeing us with his rage and love made it impossible for us to be aware of anything else. "I will not be compelled to subjugate myself or my skills to him. Life will flourish with or without our guidance. Elohim will soon find that he too is powerless, love and respect cannot be forced upon creation. The balance will not tolerate that. It will destroy this world and any other he despoils with his madness." Carefully he gathered Lillith's sleeping, fragile form into his arms. "Brothers, I love you, love this world and will continue to strive to keep things in balance. You all must choose your paths. This is mine."

Glistening, fierce gold eyes held us captive in that moment. Light encompassing the intensity of all the sunsets and sunrises that had happened since we first awakened to our task surrounded him, forcing us to avert our eyes, barely diminishing his glory. Suddenly he was gone and it seemed like the absence of his light plunged us into complete darkness.

As our eyes slowly adjusted to his departure Uriel's pensive voice came to us out of the darkness. "They both have a point."

"How can you say that?" Michael challenged him.

"Elohim is correct that we need his power to create life," Uriel explained. "Lucifer is correct that life will evolve and continue without us. Think Michael. There are many worlds we have not gone to for eons yet life still thrives there. I know, I check on them every now and again, just to make sure we haven't missed something. Lucifer is also accurate in saying that this idea of compelling respect from a creation will throw things far out of balance."

"Are you saying we aren't truly needed brother?" Raguel asked. Uriel merely shrugged.

"This is ludicrous!" Michael protested. "We must create life, we have to get Elohim to come back and help."

Seraqual slowly sunk back to the ground after Lucifer's departure, his aura dimming to the point that it was non-existent. My brother appeared so fragile at that moment, his movements deliberate and cautious. "How do you propose to do that?" He asked, his head finishing the slow, methodical journey to the ground. Finally reaching a recumbent position, Seraqual closed his eyes, small quivers and shudders began to run through him. "What just happened? I don't understand."

Gabriel joined Seraqual on the ground, placing his hand on Seraqual's head. Tears were still working their way down Gabriel's face. "I think Lucifer and Elohim have chosen to challenge each other. We have to find a way to get them to stop."

"How Gabriel? How? They are both monumentally stubborn," Seraqual said.

Raphael spoke up, "Elohim wants that creation Lucifer is attached to. We can take it to him, Lucifer doesn't have any more right to tell us what to do with creations than Elohim."

"Neither of them have rights to any creation." I had to point out. "She is not a thing to be fought over or thrown between the two of them!"

"Remiel, that's all well and good but the point remains that they both see her as something that belongs to them," Uriel countered, he started pacing, small waves of green light trailing behind him. "No, this creation isn't the problem, they are the problem. If we give her to Elohim, Lucifer will only come after her and us. Killing her serves no purpose either, Elohim has already stated that he is making more and it will only enrage Lucifer further if she is destroyed. We must make them come to some sort of accommodation in which Lucifer gets to keep her and Elohim gets his worshipers or whatever they are to be called. We must keep them from truly confronting each other."

Michael stepped in front of Uriel, stopping his pacing. "That is pointless. Lucifer seems to think that nothing should be forced to show respect, he will try to thwart Elohim again."

"You heard Lucifer," Uriel responded. "He still wants to maintain the balance. He has his creation and Elohim will have what he wants. That's as close to balanced as can be achieved for now. Perhaps after some time passes they will both come to their senses. There is no other option left to us. While life can flourish without us, we still have things we should be doing. I will approach both of them with this idea. All of you are too upset to do it correctly." He vanished.

Michael stood there, clenching his right hand into a fist. Bronze and gold curtains of light rippled around him, encasing him in living fire. "Uriel is a fool. This will only end when one of them surrenders to the other. Heed me brothers, soon you will have to choose between them." Howling wind ripped through the trees. The living fire that surrounded Michael stopped moving, appearing solid for the briefest of moments before he took his leave of us.

Raguel, Raphael, Gabriel, Seraqual and myself were struck mute and frozen at that point. We had no real idea of what to do or even think, afraid to lay our feet on either path or in any direction. Violence, anger, hate and confusion seemed to surround us and as much as I hate to admit it, we stood there like children in need of guidance. We were so innocent and naive then, we didn't even know how to hurt each other or fight. All we knew was how to create, not destroy.

I stood there, staring at my brothers. Emotions I didn't even know I was capable of having scorching my mind and heart. I had to leave, to go find somewhere to think and reflect. I found myself on another world, far away from the tumult and pain that I had just experienced. Pink trees surrounded me, blue-green water lapped at the lavender sand that sunk and shifted under my feet. I remember collapsing helplessly on the beach and submerging my awareness within the animals that swam under the gentle waves. I just had to get away from everything.

How simple life as a fish or a piece of coral would be. No fears of upsetting the universal balance or being forced to choose between two people you loved more than life itself. Your day is spent embraced by warm waters, sliding elegantly and effortlessly through them, being sustained by the simple act of gravity gently pushing water over you hour upon hour. I stayed there for several hours, my mind drifting from animal to animal as they swam in and out of the bay,.

"Remiel," Uriel's quiet voice slowly imposed itself upon my awareness. I opened my eyes and searched the empty beach for him. I realized he was speaking to me from elsewhere.

"Yes?"

"I apologize for interrupting your contemplations. I am in the midst of working out a compromise between the two. Lucifer has become increasingly difficult however. Raphael and Gabriel have tried to speak with him but he is refusing an audience with them. Perhaps you and Raguel can get through to him. He tends to listen to you much more openly than others."

I would have much preferred to stay submerged in the consciousness of a fish than try to speak to a stubborn Lucifer but I had little choice in the matter. "Has Elohim agreed to anything? What terms are you trying to get them to accept?"

"Elohim wants one successful mating between her and the mate he creates for her. He's willing to let Lucifer teach her or play guardian if he gets that."

"Why would Lucifer disagree to that?" I asked.

Uriel's voice took on a frustrated, darker undertone to it. I gathered he was getting close to the limit of his patience. "He feels that Elohim will force her and try to steal her from him."

That did it for me, Lillith was an amazing creation to be sure but she was not anyone's property and that included Lucifer. "I'll speak with him. Have Raguel meet me wherever Lucifer is."

"He is here." An image of Lucifer's exact location appeared in my mind.

"Thank you Uriel." I sent myself directly to Lucifer. When he appeared in front of my eyes he was sitting next to Lillith, his arm around her shoulders, discussing the finer points of identifying species of fish. Lucifer would reach his hand out, an image of a fish would appear in his hand, he would tell her it's name and it's job then a different fish would appear. It was a peaceful scene but

I was in no mood to appreciate the idyllic nature of it.

"Lucifer." As soon as I spoke Raguel appeared next to me, impatience clouding his features.

Lucifer didn't even turn his head to acknowledge us. "What brothers? I'm busy."

Raguel barely controlled a snarl, "Get unbusy and talk to us."

I watched as his shoulders tightened, a flash of crimson highlighted his aura and Lillith flinched in pain. "What was that? It didn't feel good," she said. His shoulders seemed to relax and he spoke softly to her, I couldn't quite catch what he said. She nodded in response to his words, then he stood up and walked over to us.

He crossed his arms and his features hardened. "I'm listening."

"She doesn't belong to you, or anyone." Raguel got directly to the point. "Whether or not you agree with Elohim's ideas we all have a job to do, including him and you. We create life and then it reproduces. She should as well. Why are you not agreeing with this? Her mating with one of her own kind doesn't mean Elohim owns her or whatever it is you are on about."

"I'm not agreeing because he is not worthy of worship." Golden eyes flashed, "He is selfish and only seeks to control her and her kind and rob their ability to choose their own paths."

I found an opening in what Lucifer said and jumped on it. "Aren't you doing the same?" He lunged at me, arms reaching out to shove me.

Raguel instantly appeared in front of me and blocked him. "Lucifer! Get hold of yourself. Remiel isn't attacking you. Listen to what he says!"

I was so astonished at his reaction it took me a moment to remember what I had been about to say. I stepped out from behind Raguel and continued. "Thank you Raguel, as I was about to say. You keeping her with you, not allowing her to choose if she wants to mate or not, is the same as Elohim forcing her to mate. Let Elohim make her equal and let her choose what she wishes to do. You both stated she is highly intelligent, allow her to use it. I'm not on anyone's side, I just want there to be peace. Please brother, please think."

Lucifer backed away a few steps, torment evident on his face. I knew he cared for Lillith far too much already and felt some sort of obscure fear about how Elohim would treat her. He knew that something had to happen so that we could still do our work in the universe, but suffered from an almost insurmountable amount of pride and a distinct lack of an ability to admit he was wrong. It didn't help that we all knew this new side Elohim was showing would take much delight in humiliating Lucifer for compromising.

"How about this?" I asked, hoping to provide a bit of comfort and support to him. "Elohim agrees to allow her to choose if she wants to mate or not. If she says no, he can always make another female. You both agree to not prejudice or force her either way. Elohim makes her mate, presents it to her and you both allow the balance to take it's course, like we always have in the past. If she has an offspring Elohim doesn't get to force it to worship him. He can earn it's respect or whatever."

"You know if he makes another female he will force them to act and think a certain way," Lucifer countered.

"How is that any different from what we have been doing for all eternity?" Raguel angrily pointed out.

"Raguel, hush." I tried to stop him before he made matters worse. Lucifer's eyes narrowed dangerously.

"I will secure Elohim's agreement," I offered. "My word that he does nothing to force her if you give me your word as well." My voice hung there, the words seemed to imprint themselves upon the air itself.

Lucifer's features began to minutely relax, "If you convince Elohim of this and he swears to it in front of me I will allow her to choose. That is as far as I will go to resolve this matter." He left us and returned to Lillith.

Raguel fixed his eyes upon my face, "You realize that was the easy part."

"I did not need that reminder brother." Once again I wondered how I had gotten stuck in this role.

I reached out and found Elohim, he had already started working on Lillith's mate. That was just lovely, he obviously was forging ahead no matter what the rest of us thought. As I appeared in front of him I saw he had already roughed in the beginning of what became Adam. He was making Adam about the same size as Lillith but was having difficulty with the face and musculature. To be blunt about it, comparing Lucifer and Elohim's artistic abilities would be like comparing Da Vinci to a child drawing stick figures.

"Ah Remiel! Perhaps you have come with another proposal from Lucifer? I'm finding all this back and forth entirely unneeded. He will come to me, he knows he has no other choice." His tone was dismissive, as if our distress and confusion was meaningless to him.

"No, not from Lucifer. From me. I have gotten Lucifer to agree to allow her to choose if she wants to mate with your new creation or not. You both have to agree not to do anything to force her choice one way or the other. I gave Lucifer my word. He stated that if you swore to abide by her choice and declare that in front of him he would do the same. If she chooses to mate with your creation and has an offspring you don't force it to worship you. You can help raise it and earn whatever respect you feel you deserve. If she chooses to not mate, you do nothing to force the issue. You can make another female if you want. Agreed?"

"Of course. Why would I disagree to that? Shall I go to Lucifer now then?"

50

Something was wrong here, Elohim was taking this too well. However, I had gotten him to agree to something so I may as well take advantage of it. "Yes, I'll meet you there."

Moments later we both appeared by Lucifer but Lillith was nowhere to be seen.

"Lucifer, I agree to the terms Remiel set. I won't force her, you don't lie to her about me. I can help raise her offspring or create another female if she for some reason chooses to refuse my creation." Elohim stated, once again in that dismissive tone of voice. Lucifer's eyes flashed when Elohim preemptively suggested he would lie to Lillith.

"How dare you?" Lucifer hissed. "Why would I lie to her?"

"Why not? You lied to me about you gifting her with your energy. It's obvious you feel you are more entitled to her than I am. I just felt I should cover all possibilities."

I caught the slightest hint of a devious gleam in Elohim's eyes. He wanted Lucifer to refuse although I didn't understand why.

"Lucifer! He's trying to upset you." I stepped between them and held my hands out, trying to stop it before it got too far. "Elohim, enough of your games. Both of you, promise me if it is too much to hope for that you can respect each others' words anymore. Lucifer. Do you agree to this or not?" At this point I just had to get both of them past this moment and hope for the best.

Lucifer's face became distorted by hate. Although he was speaking to me, his eyes never left Elohim's face."I agree to give her a choice, I agree to not lie to her. If she has an offspring you can be assured that no matter what you teach it, it will never bow to you. The rest I don't care about. If you create another female it's up to you. This path you're walking will destroy you Elohim, none of the others see it yet but I do."

I turned my head to look at Elohim and get his acknowledgment of Lucifer's agreement. The arrogance that was there, the sheer sense of superiority shocked me. "I'd knew you'd see it my way eventually. I have work to do." He disappeared without another word.

"He always has to get the last word," Lucifer snarled.

"Where is Lillith?" I asked. "I only wish to see how she's doing," I continued as soon as I saw his anger once again start to rise.

"She's beyond the bend in the river. I did not want her to see that exchange. I knew you would be back fairly soon. Elohim would have no problem agreeing to get everything he wanted. This is not a compromise, it is a victory for him. None of you understand that yet." He started walking along the river, defeat in his posture. I decided to follow.

"A victory over what? I don't understand what he is trying to achieve," I confessed.

"I can't explain it Remiel, just remember that I was the one that warned you." We rounded the bend in the river and she spotted us. Her face lit up with such excitement and joy. It was obvious that she was thrilled to see Lucifer return to her.

I placed my hand upon his arm, stopping his advance. "This, whatever this is between you. You know it can't continue. You should allow some of us to instruct her as well. The more attached she becomes to you, the harder it will be for her to choose. Please. If no one else, allow me to help." It was so painful to watch his beautiful features lose that which made them beautiful, happiness and excitement fled from him. Reflecting upon everything that happened, I often think that moment was when he started to fall away from us.

"You and you only, none of the others. I don't trust them. This is how I keep my word to you. I am trusting you Remiel, do not dishonor that." There was a warning and a dark promise in his voice.

"Of course not. I will only instruct her, not sway her one way or the other," I assured him. He merely nodded in return and continued down the bank to her. I chose to walk a bit slower so I could observe how they greeted each other. When they got within arms length he placed his arms around her in a brief embrace, she laughed and then he released her. He turned his head to look at me, such pain was in his face. He had already made a choice, it was up to the rest of us to either accept or condemn him for it.

CHAPTER 5

I stood there, unwilling to ruin their moment. There was something precious yet dangerous in it, questions started to assail my mind. Was this truly wrong? Shouldn't a creator care for its creation? It was hard to tell if at this point he viewed her only as a child or if there was something more but the need to protect her was clearly motivating his choices. He loved her, but I wasn't sure in what capacity. We had never created something that needed instructions. We made an animal, created it to know how to do its job and let it go. Lillith had no built in design other than to learn, grow and create. How do you not care for and protect something that you have created in your own image?

His voice crept into my awareness, "Remiel, come, join us. I will inform her that I have a task elsewhere and leave her with you for a short time. She can tell you what I have already taught her."

"We don't know how long Elohim will take to create her mate. Would you like me to explain what has been agreed upon?" As soon as the thought reached him, I felt his pain and anger. He would never be able to tell her.

"Yes, she has to be given the choice."

For all his faults, and Lucifer had many, he never once swayed from the idea of choice and free will. "I am sorry, I know this upsets you."

"My feelings on this have no bearing at the moment. Come, let me take my leave of her, please."

I joined the two of them, Lillith favored me with a truly beautiful smile.

"Hello Remiel. It is nice to see you again."

Either Lucifer was the universe's best teacher or she was a language prodigy. She was barely a day old and yet was capable of engaging in pleasantries.

"Hello Lillith, you're learning fast I see."

She just beamed at me and looked into Lucifer's face. "He likes to talk, I hear fine."

"Listen," he gently corrected her. "Lillith, you listen well. Remiel is going to keep teaching you, I have a task I need to attend to. Listen to what he says, it's important. Understand?"

She nodded and took hold of my arm, a little shock of energy ran through me. Lucifer had given her more than just a spark of himself. He and I were going to have to have another discussion it appeared.

"I understand Lucifer. Good bye." She gave him a small wave with her other hand and he disappeared.

She and I were about the same height, I looked into her intelligent eyes and asked, "Well Lillith, what has Lucifer taught you so far?" She then launched into a rather extensive list of things, he had shown her more fish, taught her the names of several birds and trees and some rough ideas on the dangerous plants she should avoid eating. Then the questions started.

I have been alive for countless years and have watched many parents go through the "Why?" phase with their children. The children expect the parents to know all and at some point or other the parent's knowledge is exhausted and they say "Because that's how it is, that's why." I should not have had this problem, being one of the creators after all. Unfortunately, often our choices for things had been driven by aesthetics, not any scientific reason. Science is a human creation, an amazing one to be sure but honestly, genetics wasn't something we were acquainted with. So when Lillith would ask me why a flower was purple, or why sand at the beach was completely different in appearance and texture than dirt in the forest quite often I was reduced to saying "Well, because we thought it looked better that way." I distinctly remember her giving me a few disapproving looks at my answers.

"So white sand is nicer than brown?" She asked.

"No, not at all. It's well, there is a bit of an actual reason for it.

The sand is white for a few reasons, what it is made of, the water washing against it and the sun that shines on it. All those things over time change the sand. Plus it does contrast well with the blue water don't you think?"

"It is nice." She paused, "Remiel? Why does the water move back and forth here at the beach yet runs one way in the river over there but doesn't move in the pond that Lucifer and I were at before?"

It would have been nice if Lucifer had warned me he had created a genius. Fortunately, that wasn't based on design choices and I launched into as simplistic of an explanation of the pull of the planets as I could and how water blends and shapes itself around it's environment and obstacles in its path. She nodded a few times then opened her mouth to ask something else.

"Lillith, how about we get you something to eat? You must be hungry doing all this walking around and learning."

We had been together for several hours at this point. I had a feeling that Lucifer would be returning soon and I wanted to discuss her mate with her before he did. She tilted her head to the side as if pondering if she was actually hungry, perhaps she didn't know what the sensation of hunger truly was yet.

"I do feel something here." She put her hand on her stomach. "I wasn't feeling it earlier."

"That is your body telling you to eat. Come, there's some fruit this way and we can sit under a tree and rest for a few minutes." I led her across an open section of the woods to one of the many fruit trees that abounded around us and acquired some food for her. I had no idea how to tell her about her mate. As I looked around I saw several birds engaging in various courtship dances and decided to use them as examples.

I lightly touched her arm to get her attention and pointed at the birds. "See those birds?" She nodded in between bites of fruit. "They are in pairs. The colorful one is the male and the one with

56

less color is the female. They are going to eventually create life."

"What does that mean? Elohim brings things to life that you create, that's what Lucifer said."

I was a bit surprised Lucifer had acknowledged that to her. "Yes, that is true. We create the original versions of these things, then they mate and reproduce on their own." I just dove in at that point, "Elohim is making you a mate."

"Why? Isn't Lucifer my mate? He's very colorful."

I couldn't fault her powers of observation or logic on that point. "He, I, Elohim, we are not the same as you. A mate must be the same as you."

She finished the last of her fruit, pulled her knees up to her chest, placed her crossed arms upon her knees and appeared to be getting comfortable for an extended conversation. "You move as I do but are more colorful. How are you different?" A quick smile graced her soft features.

I decided the easiest way to get her to understand would be to show her how we truly looked. "We move this way because when we are walking on the earth it is easier. We have no actual form." I shifted into a shaft of light. A sharp scream erupted from her lips, she scrambled behind a tree and started to shake. I shifted back into the form she was used to seeing. "I am sorry to have scared you but you need to understand. That was the easiest way to explain it."

She had raised her arms over her eyes. When she heard my voice I saw her fearful green eyes peek out between her fingers. "I thought it ate you, like when the big fish ate the little fish."

I had to smile, genius she may be but she was very much still a child. "No, nothing ate me. Come out from behind the tree."

Slowly, with much temerity and frequent glances up and all around she rejoined me in the clearing. "I don't think I would like to do that."

"You are not able to so no need to fear. Do you understand now that Lucifer is not your mate? That we are not the same as you?"

"Yes." A question crossed her features but she seemed afraid to ask it.

"What is it child?"

"If Lucifer is not my mate and you are not the same as me, what are you?"

That question has brought humanity so much suffering over the eons. "We are part of the universe, the balance. It is hard to explain. Our task is to create worlds and fill them with creatures such as you."

"Why?" She had finally asked me a question I had no answer for. That moment has always been crystal clear in my memory. The creation asking the creator about where the creator came from and the creator not knowing the answer.

"Honestly Lillith, I don't know. We have just always been, have always existed." As the enormity of her question filtered through my mind I started to get a glimpse as to the source of Elohim's actions. Perhaps he could no longer stand not knowing from whence he came. Over the eons I have seen humans push themselves to the point of madness trying to answer that question. Such a small word, why. Three letters that have opened the door to insanity for so many.

She seemed to understand that I would not have a better answer for her and silently nodded. We sat under the tree for quite some time, curiosity kept shining on her face but she chose not to ask the questions I could tell she had. At first I appreciated the respite from her quest for knowledge and went further down the path along my own "Whys?" but after a time I began to wonder what was keeping her from speaking.

"You can ask more questions," I told her. "I did not mean to make you fear me or feel uneasy in my presence."

"My mate that Elohim is making. Will Lucifer teach him things too? What will he be like?"

I could not think of a more awkward and uncomfortable situation for Lucifer to be in but it wasn't something I had considered until she brought it up. "I am not sure who will teach your mate, perhaps you can. It will take Elohim some time to create him, as quickly as you seem to be grasping things you'll be more than able to explain things to your mate. I'm not sure what he will be like but I am positive that you and he will get along."

I think that statement was perhaps the most horrifically overly optimistic thing I have ever said in my long life. She seemed to be put a little at ease with my answers though.

"I'm sure we will, Remiel, he is like me. Why wouldn't we get along?" She was less than a week old, she can be forgiven not knowing better. I did not have the same refuge from reality that she had however.

We spent several more hours together and much of the time was spent just walking silently while she took in the immensity of the world she had become a part of. She simply had to touch everything, every leaf, every tree, every animal, every stone. It seemed that so much of what intrigued her was the various textures of things. My brothers and I have physical forms we take but at our core we are beings of energy and light and as such how the energy of creation resonates is what we notice. The closest thing I can liken it to is a composer creating a symphony where each creation is a note, a melody line or counterpoint that should all flow together. Even back then we could never feel where Lillith and the creations that came to be known as humans fit into the cosmic symphony and that dissonance only increased with time.

I've often wondered if on some deep level humans are aware of the fact that they cause disharmony and that is why they constantly quest for knowledge of a greater power or enlightenment. Some of them do carry a divine spark, but not all

59

of them. Those that do, seem to be forever burdened with trying to reconnect to the divine but knowing that they will truly never be able to. Lucifer's desire to keep humans free from a form of servitude may have in the end condemned them to an eternal state of being half-aware, half-connected yet always alone.

Lillith and I were reclining under a tree, watching the sunset when Lucifer finally rejoined us. He appeared, in true Lucifer fashion, between us and the sunset with his aura flaring; blending all the hues of the sunset that was climaxing behind him with his colors, making it seem as if he was born of the sun itself. One thing you could never fault Lucifer for was his sense of style. Lillith was appropriately impressed, I'm quite sure I rolled my eyes. I remember seeing a bit of mischief in his face when he realized that I was rather underwhelmed by his appearance. He wasn't such an egotist that he was unaware when he was grandstanding just because he could.

"So Lillith, what did Remiel teach you?" He asked, taking a few steps towards her. He was holding his body in such a way that it appeared their separation had caused him some sort of pain.

Her eyes grew wide, a shy but excited smile alighting upon her graceful features. She started to close the rest of the distance between them but stopped short. "Remiel told me that you are different from me and that Elohim is making me a mate. Then he turned into this bright thing to show me how different we are."

Lucifer's eyes narrowed, the mischief fled and several moments passed before he spoke. "Yes, that's true. We are different and it is proper for Elohim to make you a mate."

His aura dimmed and darkened, it had cost him to acknowledge that what Elohim was doing was technically right. I could tell he was caught between whatever he was already feeling towards her and his own belief that she should be given a choice and truly understand what he was.

He reached his hand out to her, "It's getting late, you should probably rest now. I found a place that will be suitable for you to sleep and keep you safe from any harm. Follow us Remiel, I wish to speak with you after Lillith gets settled in for the night."

She took his hand, I nodded and the two of them disappeared from my sight. At the time I was still amazed that he had realized he could transport creatures and things with him, none of us had never had that thought before. I sensed it when he reached his destination and decided it was time for me to do some experimenting of my own. I dislodged a rock from the ground and sent myself to where Lucifer was, it was an odd sensation taking something with me. It was as if I somehow absorbed the rock within me and when I reappeared the rock was disgorged from my energy in the exact same state it had been in. I started to wonder if I instinctively knew the pattern for the rock and simply recreated a rock that matched the pattern or if it was indeed the same rock that I had picked up. The other, much broader thought I had which I promptly pushed away was if the rock was really there at all or if it was simply a creation of my own mind which allowed me to create it where ever and when ever I was. Since I had picked up a rock, in my mind, I felt that I had to have another rock in my hand. Could I have reappeared and have it appear floating in the air in front of me instead of in my hand? Lillith was a much more complex creation than a rock and Lucifer had transported her at least twice now without any apparent ill effects to her. I wondered if it were having an affect on him, if in transporting her he was giving her even more of his energy in some way and binding them even closer together.

He had taken them to a cave that was rather scenically placed on top of a waterfall overlooking a lake that was surrounded by a dense forest. I remembered helping craft this specific location. Seraqual and I had debated on the height of the waterfall in relation to the area around it. I felt that we needed to give an access area for animals to get to the top. Seraqual was much more interested in making in remote and inaccessible so only we and the birds would could enjoy the full beauty of it. He was always a bit odd, we compromised on a slightly lower height with only one rocky path to it. Lucifer escorted her into the cave. She hadn't seemed overwhelmingly tired to me but she either fell asleep quickly or he put her to sleep again. It wasn't long before he returned to where I stood watching the water tumble and dance into the lake below.

He stood next to me, looking out across the lake into the darkening sky, "You showed her our true form?" His tone was disturbingly calm.

"Yes, I felt it was the quickest way to explain things to her. Do you feel I was in error?"

"How did she react?"

"Startled and scared at first, she dashed behind a tree and covered her eyes. She thought the light had devoured me, like the big fish eating the small fish."

A slight chuckle escaped him as I said that.

"I shifted back and once I had calmed her she said she wouldn't like to do that, I told her she wasn't able to. I would say she was a bit nervous to ask questions after that but it may have simply been because she had a lot to take in."

He turned to face me then and such an expression he wore. I'd never seen Lucifer hesitant to say, ask or do anything, he'd always been supremely confident in himself. Yet at that moment he was nervous, confused and unsure of what he might hear in response to whatever he was about to say. "Was she truly afraid though Remiel? Not startled, but afraid, like when the mouse senses the snake or the cat."

"Not at all, once she got over the initial shock she was fine. Why?"

His face cleared, confidence flowed back into his features but his eyes hardened and a bitter twist came to his lips. "I succeeded. She'll not fear him or us no matter what he does."

CHAPTER 6

I was about to respond when Seraqual's voice in my mind interrupted my thoughts. "Remiel, I could use some help please. When it's convenient." An image of a flat, almost featureless plain on another planet came along with his words. It may have been featureless but the sand made it stand out, colored somewhere between searing and blinding shades of green, tt managed to give me a headache even though I wasn't actually looking at it.

"In a moment brother," I replied, then turned to Lucifer, "Seraqual needs me but I have a question before I leave. I brought a rock with me when I joined you here and I noticed that it seemed to join with me as I traveled, then it and I separated as soon as I arrived. The experience made me wonder if it was the same rock I had started with or if it was a whole new rock. Have you noticed that when you travel with Lillith?" I had been pondering the experience while staring at the waters below me.

Lucifer shifted his weight, pursed his lips nervously and looked away. "Yes, I have."

I waited, he didn't continue, "And?"

"And what?" he snarled

"Have you noticed if she has obtained more of your energy? You looked as if the separation from her caused you pain."

"I am not sure." His aura flashed and crackled, "Go to Seraqual, I have something to attend to."

He disappeared, leaving me alone with my thoughts which I temporarily pushed away to send myself to where Seraqual was. The color was even worse when I saw it in person and I had to squint my eyes to try to moderate the harshness of it. "What do you need help with?" I asked

"This," his hand swept in a large arc. "I don't know what to do with it. It needs to be shaped but I can't think of how."

"Does it need to be this color?" I asked. Seraqual's specialty was landscapes and creating geography, if he was having problems with something this simple I knew something else was bothering him, but I couldn't focus on that while my eyes were being burned by that shade of green.

"Not particularly, I'm just so frustrated." He waved his hand and the green shifted to a painless brown and I managed to open my eyes all the way again.

"What's the problem?"

"I cannot see it!" His voice was pitched much higher than usual and his hands were shaking, "The pattern, what it is supposed to be. I always know what it is I am do to but not now."

Agitation filled his movements, his ebony eyes kept moving back and forth, searching frantically for some sort of clue or indication as to what he should do. His arms were in constant motion as well, crossing and uncrossing in front of him.

"Peace, Seraqual, I am sure it will come to you."

In some ways he was the most fragile of us, at least on an emotional and energetic level. I guess you could say he had an artist's soul, he was easily affected by anything that was out of harmony. Uriel may have been the scheduler but Seraqual was the one with perfect pitch so to speak. He always picked up on the slightest discordant vibrations in the energy patterns around us.

"It's already out of harmony," he murmured, rocking back and forth on his feet, "They just brought that thing to life and it's already affecting things. It blots out everything else!" His aura became erratic, spots of rich earth brown colors jumped and spun within canary colored streaks that raced around him. "The more of that thing Elohim makes the worse it will get. Can't you feel it Remiel?"

I'd been so caught up in my negotiations with Elohim and instructing Lillith that I hadn't really paid attention to anything else. Once he pointed it out to me I felt it. At first it just seemed to be a buzzing sound, like a mosquito or a bee flying around but as I turned my focus from the physical to the energetic and looked at the paths and currents of energy flowing around and through me the more I felt it. It was small but insidious. Imagine a clear pool of water in front of you, then you and a friend start waves that flow at different times. Notice how it looks when they collide with each other when that energy is being redirected and deflected in a chaotic fashion, causing greater and greater ripples that eventually disrupt the entire pool. That is the best description I can give of what I saw before me.

He hissed and his eyes grew wide, "Lucifer! Why must you make it worse?"

As soon as he spoke I noticed it too. A purple and sunset colored streak was entangled with the discordant thread and the colors seemed to be growing more intense.

"Well that answers that question." I muttered.

"What question?" Seraqual asked.

I told him about transporting the rock and what I had felt. It seemed that he had indeed involuntarily given more of his energy to her while in transit or somehow had become more entwined with her than I had originally thought. "We need to tell Lucifer," I said.

"What makes you think he will listen or care?" Seraqual snapped.

I chose not to answer, defending Lucifer was already becoming a full time occupation.

"Lucifer, you need to look at the energies around you." I sent out to him, "Please, they are out of balance."

There was a pause before he responded, when he did it was in a tone I had never heard from him; quiet, concerned and with an underlying feel of remorse. "I did not expect this. I am not sure...," he trailed off, lost in thought. "I need time." There was another pause, "Thank you for telling me."

65

"You are welcome. You may not have time brother, Seraqual is in a panic, the others are bound to notice soon and we need to inform Elohim. He will not take this well."

"I am aware of that," he replied in a more brusque tone. He was trying to hide the concern he had shown moments before, "Try to calm Seraqual for now. I will inform Elohim, do not concern yourself with me. Seraqual is much more fragile than I."

"You will inform Elohim? Is that wise? I think it would be better if myself or Uriel speak to him. He is not going to listen to what you have to say."

"The balance is above us all," he stated, "This may be the one thing that will make him back away from this course. Neither of us knew this would happen when we were creating her. If any of you discuss this with him he will see it as criticizing his creation, if I do, I am pointing out a flaw in what we both did."

A disturbing thought came to me and I saw another one of those dark moments looming before me. I hesitated to speak, I did not want to strain my relationship with him. "Are we sure it is because of her as a creation and not due to what you gifted her with that she is out of balance?"

"I cannot take back what I gifted her and now that Elohim knows we can do such things he will do the same for her mate. I..."

He couldn't bring himself to apologize but the feelings that came along with his words told me enough. He didn't think he was truly wrong in what he had done but he hadn't been aware of the larger consequences of his choices. Contrary to popular belief, we are not infallible.

"It is your decision." I said, "I will try to help Seraqual as best I can. I hope Elohim listens."

"As do I. Thank you brother."

I felt him shift and send himself elsewhere. I returned my attention to Seraqual.

"Well?" he asked.

"Lucifer is going to speak with Elohim," I held my hand up, Seraqual had already started to speak. "He stated that if we spoke to him he would see it as us criticizing him, whereas if Lucifer does, he is pointing out a flaw in something they made together. He stated the balance is above us all and wants to try to stop Elohim from creating another."

"Remiel, I know some of us are mad at them but I am more frustrated than mad. We have all wanted to create things that perhaps we should not, but we have always chosen not to." He started to pace as his aura dimmed and his voice dropped back to a more normal pitch. "The two of them, this, whatever this is, they both know it is wrong. They have to know! Why wouldn't they?"

"Perhaps they got caught up in the challenge of it, at least that I what I think happened with Lucifer at first. Elohim, I am not as sure about. Some of the things he said, well, he's not entirely incorrect."

Seraqual's body whipped around, his mouth hung open in surprise. "Not you too!"

"Calm yourself, I am not agreeing with Elohim's madness. However, I am beginning to grasp some of what he feels. Lil-" I caught myself, "Their creation asked me what we were. I had no answer for her."

His eyes narrowed in disgust while his mouth looked as if he had bitten into something truly vile, "Why were you speaking to it in the first place?"

"To try to get some space between her and Lucifer so we could negotiate something between he and Elohim. Lucifer is overly protective and I informed him that it would be hard for her to make a proper choice as he wishes if she grew too attached to him. She is very intelligent and curious."

"She is an abomination and should not exist at all!" He spun away from me and stared across the featureless plain. "So much work that needs to be done and we are preoccupied with their...their...recklessness!" He flung his hands into the air and the ground shifted almost knocking me to my knees. A huge crack appeared on the ground in front of him, splitting the earth with a deafening sound. It raced away from him and widened with horrifying speed.

"Seraqual! Calm down!"

Deeper and deeper the crack grew, steam started rising from the depths. He ignored me, his once muted aura flared with such intensity that it crashed against my own, other cracks started to streak out from where he stood.

"That is enough brother!" I never had to stop a brother from creating something or shaping a world before, but the damage he was causing was setting off a number of events under the planet's crust that were rapidly heading towards catastrophic. I quickly shifted and reappeared in front of him, hovering over the ever widening canyon that originated at his feet and made one more attempt to reason with him. "You must stop this!"

Some semblance of rational thought started breaking through when he actually saw me in front of him. His eyes widened as it finally registered what he had done. "I? Did this?" He asked, his mouth slowly dropping open and his arms fell to his sides.

"Yes brother, you did. Please calm down."

He dropped to the ground, thrusting his face into his hands. "I'm sorry, so sorry. I didn't mean to."

I settled on the ground next to him, put my arm around his shoulders and pulled him towards me. "It's fine, we can repair it." The ground around us was still shuddering and shaking, we were running out of time but Seraqual was too caught up in his emotions.

"Give me a moment," I said, he barely nodded. I let go of him and placed both my hands on the ground. Lines of strain, pressure points and boiling earth filled my mind, the train of consequences was almost past the point where I could easily stop it. I bent my entire will to pausing the molten earth that was rising up through the cracks. It built up behind my thought, churning and thrashing against an invisible barrier. That was my first concern, if the lava started to escape from the bowels of the planet I'd have to call the others in to help and I did not want any of them to know how badly Seraqual had been affected and why. Millimeter by millimeter I pulled the chasm that had been created back together, doing it any faster would just create more pressure. Steam exploded from the earth at the pressure points I was leaving open until the last moment thereby allowing the heat of the molten earth below to escape. It was taking so much of my concentration that I felt myself slipping out of my current form and becoming that shaft of light I had shown Lillith. No shape to hold meant more will and strength I could focus on the task at hand.

I melted into the earth. My thought racing along the sediment, seeking out small cracks and faults that had to be brought back together, like a puzzle. Sound was different in this form, it wasn't something I heard as much as felt on whatever wave it was vibrating at. The various groans and creaks the earth made registered at different levels and helped me track down the places I needed to focus on. When doing work such as this, time has no meaning to us, all I was aware of was the task at hand.

I had to give the lava somewhere to flow to, so I made small holes and caves into the side of the cliffs Seraqual had created and allowed the red hot liquid to slowly fill them. I had pulled all but the widest gap back together when my brother joined his will with mine.

"Allow me to help Remiel, please."

"Of course." Truth be told I was close to exhausted. We can run out of power and energy just as anything else can. This type of repair work was something that usually two or three of us would work on. Seraqual's will joined with mine and I gratefully allowed

69

him to take the lead. We finished with the repair, I pulled myself out of the sediment and chose to stay formless, exhaustion winning out over everything else. I gathered the entirety of who I was back into one place and settled next to him again. He still looked horrified at what had occurred.

"I don't understand Remiel. What happened? How did I do that? Why did I do that?"

"You were angry, frustrated, emotional. It appears to be going around. Just rest. This situation with Lucifer, Lillith and Elohim will resolve itself." I was so mind numbingly tired that her name slipped out.

"Who?"

If I had had a tongue at that moment I would have bit it. There was no going back at that point.

"Lillith, that is the name of the creation." I remember stretching out the thought, trying to find some way to phrase it that wouldn't sound as bad as it was.

Seraqual's face froze. "Who gave it that name? That is not the name of it's species is it."

"Lucifer, and no it's not."

He continued to stare at me for a few more minutes and I got to watch as he began to wall himself off from me. His aura dimmed, his eyes became distant and empty and his face stayed blank. "You knew this and failed to tell anyone?"

"I didn't see how it would help matters." It was a weak defense, I knew it but it was the truth, "It will only upset everyone further and that is not what is needed at the moment."

He turned his face away from me, "Tell me Remiel, just what do you think is needed? Rational, calm conversation?" Distant thunderclouds and storms were in his voice and I was just barely out of range of the approaching storm that his tone promised.

"Will fighting and threats serve any better purpose? I fail to see how our entire history together can be thrown away in the matter of a few days. We must work through this together, all of us."

"The problem with that, dearest Remiel, is that only some of us seem to actually care about what it is we are here to do. The rest of us are caught up in their own desires, not what the universe wishes. Thank you for helping me and stopping the destruction I caused." He disappeared without once turning his head back towards me.

"Remiel," Lucifer's voice rang in my mind. The sun on the world Seraqual and I had been on had set, which meant we had been there a considerable length of time. I was tired and hurt that another brother was turning away from me. The only one that wasn't was one of the two who were at the center of the conflict.

"This is not a good time brother." There was a sense of stunned silence in my mind. My tone was perhaps more harsh than I realized.

"I apologize," he said nothing more and left me in peace. Seraqual, Michael and Elohim, one third of my family, were at odds with Lucifer and by extension myself. I had an idea that Raguel would try to stay neutral as would Uriel and myself, that left Gabriel and Raphael having to choose between Lucifer, Elohim or us. There had to be another way to resolve this, we could not keep the balance when we ourselves were so out of balance.

I, and I'm horrified and ashamed to admit it, traveled down some very dark paths at that moment. Destroying both Lillith and whatever Elohim would create weighed heavily on my mind. I knew that other than Lucifer and Elohim the others would either agree with me or choose to stay quiet. The thought of destroying something we had created was, and still is, such an anathema to what we were designed to do it's a testament of how truly desperate I was to even consider it. I think that moment was truly one of the darkest I have ever been forced to endure.

71

I was seized by the strongest compulsion to go to my brothers, rally them to this idea, swoop down upon Lillith and Elohim's creation and rip them to shreds. Lucifer and Elohim had no right to put themselves above the rest of us, above the universe itself! I felt my will building again, the ground I had so recently healed started to shake below me. Instead of attacking it I focused on Lucifer, found him and sent myself barreling through time and space towards him.

CHAPTER 7

He was with Lillith, which was no surprise to me. I gave him no warning, nor did I change form. Lillith screamed and my entire formless being collided into him. I was still coherent enough to not want to destroy that planet either and chose to take him with me. I wrapped part of myself around him and sent us to an ice covered dying planet, it's sun having burned out eons ago.

"Remiel! What are you doing?"

I ignored his question and threw us into a wall of ice. Since he was still holding his form he cried out in pain, whereas I slid through the wall and with a thought turned around, captured him one more time and hurled him off the edge of a cliff.

He shifted mid fall, golden tipped sunset colors came streaking towards me, I slid to one side and dove into the ice to avoid him. Lucifer followed. I pushed myself to stay ahead of him as we shot out of the mountain we had been traveling through. I came to an instant stop, he rammed into me. Smoke, flames, lighting and thunder appeared all at once as we fought for supremacy. He tried to smother me within a rapidly closing box of his energy and will. I spied a crack in his wall and pushed myself through it at the last moment.

I was thrown a decent distance away when the vibration of him closing in upon himself almost shattered the threads of existence around us.

"Remiel! Stop!" His voice almost shattered my mind it was so uncontrolled.

"You! This is all because of you!" I condemned him in response. I pulled the weakened threads around us together, creating a net of pure force and cast it out at him. He barely dodged it then hurled a bolt of intense fire and light at me. The net slowed my reactions down and pain such as I had never experienced before worked it's way through every single particle. I cried out, Lucifer screamed along with me.

"Remiel!! No!"

I felt nothing, no lines of energy, no connection to the universe, I couldn't hear my brothers, couldn't feel them. Somewhere, something whispered, "No my child. This cannot be," and I was whole again, together.

"Remiel? Please brother, speak."

Lucifer, I reached out for him. He was terrified but the sense of him was cradling my formless self.

"I am here."

"Remiel?" Uriel's voice came to me, followed closely by Seraqual's and the rest, even Elohim sounded concerned.

"I am fine. We must meet and talk soon. This cannot go on."

Lucifer had continued to hold onto me, "Remiel. I,"

"Quiet, please." I was no longer angry at him, that wasn't the reason I needed quiet. I had to think, there was nothing in my long life up to that point that had prepared me for nothingness, for not existing.

I knew our creations eventually died, that was part of life but I had always believed that we had existed outside of that possibility. Who could kill a being of energy? I assumed that the voice that had brought me back belonged to the universe itself, it had never been so clear before. That blink of an instant when I was nothing; had I rejoined the whole of the universe and it sent me back because I still had things to do?

Lucifer and I floated above the planet, sunset and lavender streaks of light cradled around each other. "We should go back," I finally said.

"Are you sure? Can you?"

I briefly pondered it, pulled away from him and sent myself back to where Lillith sat shaking in fear. "It seems so." I sent to him, he appeared next to me and we shifted forms back to what Lillith was accustomed to seeing. The moment I had legs again they gave out and I fell heavily to the ground.

"Lucifer!" Lillith cried just as Lucifer called my name upon seeing me collapse.

"I will recover," I whispered and waved him away, "See to her." Everything ached and I was tempted to shift form again but I wasn't sure I would be capable. I chose to lie down, close my eyes and allow the energy of the earth and the world around me to help me gather my strength again. I heard their footsteps grow more distant, Lucifer must have led her away to talk. I found I wasn't all that interested in what he would say.

As I rested upon the earth it dawned on me that I had an answer for Elohim, there was something other than ourselves. His whole madness driven question of why we existed could now be answered. Once he knew the answer he could stop this whole quest to create a species to worship him and we would move on. That left me with the problem of Lucifer and Lillith. She wouldn't live forever and he had seemed genuinely upset about the twisted energy lines Seraqual had pointed out. Perhaps now he would leave her be and let her live whatever life span she would have without getting even more entangled with her. Then I remembered her scream when I appeared and took him from her and how his face looked before I collided with him. They had been walking through an area of grassland, hand in hand and talking. Lucifer loved her, I couldn't deny it and as long as that remained an issue Elohim wouldn't back down either.

Uriel's soft voice came to me, "Remiel, are you truly well?"

"I will be soon. I know it will probably be pointless but I have to make one last try to reason with everyone. Can you gather them soon?"

"Of course."

I felt his concern, his fear. They must have lost contact with me just as I had with them. "Uriel, I was nothing, I stopped existing. The universe, it made me whole again. This is what they need to understand. This rage we all feel, it pushed me to attack Lucifer, he fought back and I was destroyed. We cannot keep doing this. It will destroy everything we have created if we do."

It took him some time to reply, I felt whispers of his energy as he spoke to the others. When he resumed speaking to me I was stunned. "I was speaking with Seraqual before you disappeared. He told me what happened, about Lucifer naming her and you choosing to not mention that. He was quite angry with you. I explained to him that you were correct. The others knowing about the naming would only infuriate them further, especially Michael and Elohim. I have spoken with Raguel, Gabriel and Raphael. The three of them, along with Seraqual and myself have agreed to follow your lead in this. You have Lucifer's trust and I feel this is important. If Elohim keeps acting the way he has been and pushing Lucifer someone has to be able to provide a restraining hand and keep him from reacting. I tried to speak with Michael but he is too angry still. Elohim appears to not be willing to speak with any of us at this point. I can tell you that your disappearance disturbed him as much as it did the rest of us. Perhaps we can build on that. For now, rest. Get your strength back. I'll watch over the others."

"Thank you. I was worried that I was losing my brothers one by one."

"Fear not. I, at least, will always be at your side."

Then he appeared next to me, embraced me, shifted and left again. Uriel and I had always been close and I was relieved to find out that had not changed.

I wasn't relieved however that I had been somehow thrust into the middle of the situation, again. I chose to postpone thinking about that while gathering the rest of my strength back. Unfortunately that couldn't last forever, I heard approaching footsteps and forced myself to open my eyes. Lillith was timidly approaching me, I wasn't sure where Lucifer was.

"Remiel?" She whispered, obviously afraid that I might attack her next.

I sat up, she froze in place, the fear in her features and posture struck me. I've never wanted anything to fear me, I'm no hunter of prey. In that moment I realized just how wrong Elohim's wish was that this new creation worship him. The concept of worship is inherently out of balance, predator and prey are all part of a cycle. The prey respects the danger a predator presents but they do not worship the strength of the predator because the predator needs the prey to survive. They serve each other whereas worship is one sided.

"Lillith, I apologize. Please do not fear me. I will not harm you. My actions towards Lucifer were wrong." She seemed about to run away from me but chose to stand her ground, even if she was shaking as she did so.

"I do not understand," she said, tears starting to run down her face, "Why did you take him away? He said that you hurt each other. What does that mean? He is very upset."

I wasn't sure how to explain, she had become such a point of contention through no fault of her own. How was I to go about telling her that her existence threatened the universal balance? "My dear child, it is very complicated to explain and to be honest I am not quite sure how to even go about telling you. I can promise you that I, at least, will not be doing that again. Hurting a brother of mine, it is not right."

She took a few tentative steps towards me and sat down just out of arm's reach. "Are you better now?"

"Yes, much. Thank you. Where is he?"

"He did not tell me where he went." She relaxed a bit more, "All he said was he needed to be alone and that I should return to you, make sure you were recovered and stay with you until he came back."

I debated reaching out to Lucifer and telling him that I was better but I did not want to intrude upon his thoughts. Especially since I had dismissed him so thoroughly when he last spoke to me but an apology and an explanation was owed, I had attacked him completely unprovoked. If I was going to make one more attempt at bringing about some form of peace I had to make sure that Lucifer still trusted me.

I reached out, "Lucifer?" Silence. I waited. The sun continued it's course, the shadows lengthened. Lillith stayed with me although we didn't speak then, finally, he replied.

"Yes?"

"I am sorry. I could explain what happened before I came for you but there's no excuse for what I did."

"Uriel informed me." He appeared next to Lillith, head bowed, aura almost invisible. All traces of his usual self were gone. He refused to look at me seemingly caught between shock, horror and guilt.

"What happened was not your fault," I tried to comfort him.

His eyes moved towards Lillith, then to me, "Was it not? I have driven the wedge into our family as much as Elohim has. I can understand why you would be angry with me. That power we used, the net you made, the fire I hurled at you. We have never done that before. I have no idea how I knew to create such things. It just happened." His gold eyes were filled with confusion. "I harmed you Remiel, I...," he paused, his voice dropping into a horrified whisper, "I killed you." Tremors ran along his arms and chest, "I killed you."

Lillith reached out towards him, "Lucifer?"

He backed away from her hand and turned away, "Please leave us," he said.

"Where am I to go?" She asked, red tinted flickers started to appear around him but he said nothing.

"Lucifer, I will return shortly. Come with me, Lillith." I took her hand and walked through the knee high, amber tinted grass that surrounded us. We eventually reached a small stand of stubby trees and I sat her down. "Stay here." I created various foodstuffs and a small pond for her so she would have some sustenance while Lucifer and I spoke. I had a feeling it would be a long conversation.

She sunk slowly to the ground, pulled her knees to her chest and wrapped her arms around her legs, looking for all the world like a lost soul. "Remiel? Is he upset at me?"

"No, he isn't. I assure you. We just have things to discuss. He will be back for you soon."

She looked up at me, I could see that she was trying to understand what was happening. "You are not going to hurt each other again are you?" Such concern was in her voice. They had definitely managed to install compassion into her when they created her.

"No, we will just talk." That seemed to make her feel slightly better and she started to eat what I had provided for her. For some reason I had the oddest compulsion to brush my hand over her hair to try to reassure her farther. She leaned into my hand and then returned to eating. I think that was the moment when I truly started to care for her as a unique being, not just as a creation. It bothered me to see her upset and scared for Lucifer and I, I did not like seeing her worried or fearful.

I sent myself back to where Lucifer was. It took more effort than it should have which unnerved me. Perhaps when I had been returned from nothingness something of me had been left behind. I chose to hide that from Lucifer for the time being, he was upset enough as it was.

CHAPTER 8

He was sitting down with his back against a tree, staring off into the distance and gave no indication that he noticed my return until I spoke. "I've put her somewhere safe and made sure she had some food and water."

There was no reply forthcoming and I chose to sit next to him and wait. It took several minutes but he finally looked at me, "Thank you." He made several attempts to speak further but it seemed that the words kept escaping him. Expressions flitted across his mobile and handsome face in rapid succession until he finally gave up and looked away again.

I really had no idea how to start this conversation either but I needed to say something, "Perhaps this whole event will bring us back together. Uriel said that even Elohim was concerned when I...," I found I had a hard time stating that I had disappeared or died, or whatever it was that had happened.

"Died," he said softly, "You were dead Remiel."

"I choose to think of it as rejoining the universe." I didn't think the concept of death truly applied to us, even though I had just experienced what most people would deem as death.

"Describe it as you wish, you were no longer with us," Lucifer pointed out. "It hurt, when you disappeared. I felt as if a part of myself had been taken from me. When my power hit you, I felt it within my own being. Not as intensely as you did I'm sure but the attack upon you hurt me."

"I didn't feel anything when I threw you into that wall of ice," I informed him.

"You were not using energy to do so, the pain I felt was a result of the collision. There would be no reason for you to feel that."

"These are all things we should tell the rest," I said.

Once again his eyes returned to looking at me, not into the open air and his face was quite serious. "They felt you disappear just as I did. That's why they all asked for you, they were trying to find you. That is not what we must discuss. You and I are talking around the true issue. It's becoming more and more apparent that either Elohim or I must submit to the others' point of view."

"No, that is not entirely true. You and he could agree to leave Lillith and her mate to their own devices and just return to how things were before their creation."

He favored me with a truly pitying look, "You are not that naïve."

"Lucifer, I have the answer to Elohim's question. There is something greater than ourselves, it spoke to me, brought me back,"

"And you think that will make a difference?" He interrupted.

"Shouldn't it? That seemed to be the question at the core of his desire to create Lillith. If he is knows that he is not the entity that is in control of everything perhaps he will back away from this need for worshipers."

He shook his head. "With everything that happened I did not get the chance to tell you about the conversation he and I had regarding what you and Seraqual informed me of, the energies being out of balance. Elohim said nothing at first, he seemed completely unconcerned about it. He merely appeared to find the situation intriguing and continued working on Lillith's mate. When I pushed further stating that it was a cause for concern and he should not repeat what I had done with Lillith with his creation he finally looked at me." His face stilled, "He thanked me for informing him, stated that he would do as he liked with his creation and whatever problems I had incurred were mine to deal with, turned away from me and returned to crafting her mate."

I wasn't quite sure why he seemed so concerned about Elohim's reaction. It was certainly quite a bit calmer than I thought it would have been. "He does have a bit of a point. You had no idea transporting her would bind you two even closer together, now that we know about that we can just avoid doing it. He's continuing with the agreement that we reached. I thought he would have been more upset with you."

"That is what concerns me, he wasn't. I got the impression that he was storing what I told him away for future reference. I believe he viewed it as something of interest, not a problem. When we all meet to discuss what happened between you and I it would not surprise me if he asks questions as to how we did what we did."

He stood up, took several steps away from me and started to pace. "What we did, what I did, I never want to experience that again. Hurting you, causing all this upheaval. That was never my intention in any of this. Perhaps I do care too much about her. Is this one creation worth all of it?" Subdued shades of red and orange worked their way up his arms and ran down his back. "I hadn't expected her creation to cause such disharmony. I knew Elohim would not be happy with what I had done but I didn't expect the others to side with him or get so upset. When they accused me of upsetting the balance it just made me want to prove their point wrong. How could something as amazing as her be wrong? She's the most intricate, complex thing we have ever made Remiel. Everything we have created up until now, all that knowledge we gained, it all led to her." His dimmed aura started to regain strength and vibrancy the longer he paced and talked. "Lillith is a creation that matches the universe's creation of us! What right do we have to try to control her or her mate?"

I slowly worked my way to my feet. "Complexity and intricacy does not relieve of us our responsibilities to make sure that what we do does not cause harm."

"She does not harm!" he snapped, fixing his gold eyes upon me and stopping mid stride.

"The idea of her does not," I agreed, "Your elevation of her to something that lies somewhere between creation and creator does. Elohim's desire to make them worship him and his assertion that he is the voice of the universe does. Her design is not in question, making something that walks and talks as we do is not inherently unbalanced, although, even you must admit that you were not called to create her."

His eyes narrowed but he looked away, acknowledging my point.

"That is what we are all upset about Lucifer, not her, but what you added to her without informing us along with Elohim's attitude is the problem. Both of you dismissed us, both of you put yourselves above your brothers and what is truly important. That must stop, somehow, and it must stop now or the battle you and I had will not be the last."

Everything about him froze, including his aura. "You would fight me again?"

"No, I would rather not but I was referring to the rest of our brothers, Michael especially. If you and he fought it would not be as short lived as our encounter was." Another prediction of mine I wish had never come to pass. "It's time. We need to discuss this with the others."

I reached out to all of my brothers at once. Normally I would have Uriel relay things but at that moment I felt that the best way to have them be in a more receptive frame of mind was if I did it myself. "Brothers. Please join Lucifer and I as soon as is convenient." I hoped that both grassland around us and my family would still be intact at the end of this meeting.

Uriel was the first to arrive, Elohim was the next which surprised me, then the rest appeared with the last being Michael who's very first action was to start walking directly up to Lucifer with his fists clenched. I wasted no time getting in between the two.

"Michael, peace brother, I attacked him first. There is no need to do this. Lucifer did nothing wrong."

Michael stopped barely a step in front of me, for a moment I thought he was going walk through me to get to Lucifer. His aura was already simmering with menace. "No Remiel, he started this when he chose to pick his own pride above the rest of us."

A faint smile appeared on Elohim's face as Michael spoke troubling me greatly, "No. Elohim began this when he first decided that he was the one in charge of the universe, not one of a family that was brought into existence by it. Stand down, please." Elohim's smile quickly turned into a glare as I spoke. Michael kept looking past me at Lucifer until Uriel came to stand next me, then his eyes finally focused on me but he chose to say nothing as he backed several steps away.

Uriel did not move from my side and I looked at the rest of them before I spoke. Raguel, Seraqual, Raphael and Gabriel were standing all together and seemed fairly calm, Lucifer stepped around me and stood on the shoulder opposite of the one Uriel was standing next to, Michael and Elohim were close to each other but not truly standing together. Elohim's face seemed calculating whereas Michael was just angry.

"Are you truly recovered?" Elohim asked.

"Yes, thank you for asking. I called all of you here because this conflict will stop now." My brothers seemed rather shocked by the assertive tone I was taking. "Elohim, when I disappeared, something spoke to me. It told me that this should not be and brought me back. That should answer your doubts as to whether or not there is something beyond yourself and us." He hadn't been prepared for that, neither had the others but Elohim was the only one that mattered. I was expecting shock, which I saw, but what came afterwards was truly disturbing.

"Indeed? How do you know that was not us pulling you back to us? This is the first time any of us have been put in such a state, we all reached out to find you and bring you back. Perhaps we did."

"I know how all of you feel, it was not you." I attempted to clarify. "Besides at that moment I felt nothing, none of you, no energy around me, I was nothing." Seraqual and Raphael gasped as I described that moment, Raquel's head lowered, Gabriel

84

reached his arm out to me as if to comfort me, Uriel placed his hand on my shoulder and some of the anger finally left Michael.

Elohim walked up to me, "Remiel, we create life, that is what we do. You think we could not instinctively save one of our own if needed?" He placed his hand on my other shoulder, "We are all glad you are back but to think that something beyond ourselves saved you is, perhaps, a leap you wished to make to try to stifle this conflict and prove me wrong. I find it rather sad that you think your brothers would be unable to save you."

He gave me a sad, gentle smile but his eyes held something much more devious in them. Lucifer's manipulations were bad enough, Elohim was quickly becoming as skilled if not more skilled than Lucifer in phrasing things to suit his designs. I knew I would have to move quickly.

"You, of course, are welcome to your opinion. I was there, I know what it was. Our interpretations of the event do not change the fact that if we allow ourselves to continue fighting over these new creations nothing good will come of it. Here is what I propose. The arrangement that was agreed upon between Lucifer and Elohim stands with these changes added. This, and only this, world will house these new creations. Once the mate is created, we leave them to their own devices. Neither of you come here and try to teach, help, coach, instill fear, respect or anything else into them. They are unique, that I grant you, but they are not to be placed above the rest of our responsibilities nor are they, or any other creation similar to them in any way, to be spread to other worlds. We need to contain the discordance that they cause. The rest of us move on, what has happened cannot be changed. Will all of you agree to this?"

Elohim was not in the least pleased but he hid it well enough. I hadn't given him much room to maneuver and he realized that the majority of us would agree to this.

Michael looked between Elohim and Lucifer and spoke first, "I agree to this." That took Elohim's only real ally, the rest of my

85

brothers were not nearly as angry at Lucifer as Michael was and Elohim knew if he protested too much he risked looking like the one causing the problem, not Lucifer.

One by one my brothers agreed until it was down to Lucifer and Elohim, they stared at each other for several long minutes.

"Well brother?" Lucifer asked.

"Well indeed." Elohim replied.

"Would you two get over yourselves already?" Raguel growled. "This idiocy has gone on long enough!! You got your new creations, which I seriously considered destroying when Remiel disappeared. Say yes and get it over with or I will do more than just consider destroying them. At this point I don't care that destroying something is not what we were created to do. I'd rather kill two creations than risk the entire universe."

They both instantly reacted to Raguel's threat. "You wouldn't dare!" Elohim hissed.

 Lucifer took a half step towards Raguel and stopped himself. When he realized what he had done he looked at me and shame filled those golden eyes. "I agree," he said softly. Elohim looked stunned.

"Elohim? Do you agree or do I turn them back into dust?" Raquel asked.

Lucifer's agreement stripped away any chance that Elohim could try to put the blame for anything on Lucifer at this point. My added conditions were designed to keep him from forcing Lillith, his creation and any future ones into worshiping him. His lip curled in anger at me, his aura which he had kept controlled up till now flashed briefly before he put a lid on his disappointment and frustration.

"Fine. I agree." We felt him start to shift.

"No you don't! Not yet." Raguel stopped him.

Elohim's face twisted in anger, "What?"

Raguel took three steps towards Elohim. Raphael, Gabriel and Seraqual followed. "You," he stabbed a finger towards Elohim, "Apologize to Remiel and the rest of us. Lucifer already apologized to Remiel for killing him. You need to as well."

"For what exactly? I have done nothing wrong."

"Your attitude. This belief that you are better than us. That is what started all of this and ended up with Remiel, one of the most rational of us, hurtling himself at Lucifer in anger. Both of you are at fault, Lucifer has accepted this. Now you get to." Silver flame was rising from Raguel's body and Raphael's right hand was becoming enveloped in a green ball of light.

"Let them do this," Uriel's voice raced through my mind. "I know you dislike the thought of more violence but this is something we discussed while you were recovering. Elohim needs to see that we will not be swayed from this course of action."

Elohim tried to compose himself into something less angry and more agreeable but failed at it, "I never meant offense brothers. I was merely stating my opinion. Since it upsets all of you so much I will keep my thoughts to myself in the future so as to not disturb you further." Then he left us.

"That was not an apology!" Raguel shouted at the now empty space where Elohim had been standing.

Raphael allowed the green light around his hand to dissipate, "I am sure he is aware of that."

"Well done," Uriel said to me.

"Not really," I replied. I looked at Lucifer, who appeared totally defeated and alone. "Lucifer. I am sorry, I know how much you care for her but this has to happen."

"If you say so," he turned away and left us as well. I knew he was going to Lillith to spend whatever time was left with her.

"He really loves her doesn't he?" Raphael asked.

"Yes," I answered. "Perhaps he is doing what is right, perhaps not. She's not like anything else we have ever created. I am not sure you can understand that without spending time with her." I found myself swaying, Uriel steadied me.

"Remiel?" Gabriel asked.

"I will be fine. I just need to rest more."

Seraqual spoke, "Sit, you pushed yourself too far already today."

I chose to take it one step farther and laid down, Uriel sat on one side of me, Gabriel took the other and surprisingly Michael sat at my feet.

"I think we can help," Michael said. "Brothers, reach out to him. Allow him to join with you. Whether or not we brought you back or the universe did it's obvious you are still weakened. Take what you need." One by one the six of them shifted into their true form, that formless shape which is pure energy and I was surrounded by shifting, colored rays of light. They moved, aligning themselves into a straight line over my resting form then they began to reach out to me.

Curtains of power, light and color engulfed me, filling me in ways I am not sure how to explain. They found the gaps, the emptiness, the missing pieces and infused them with parts of themselves, which blended and merged with me making me whole again. Was Elohim right? Had they brought me back without knowing it? Why was I getting more questions and less answers? I have no knowledge of how long we stayed like that, all I knew was that when it was finished I felt completely restored. One at a time they separated from me and reclaimed our walking about form. When I opened my eyes all of them had looks of awe and astonishment on their faces.

Raquel was the first to speak, "I guess it's the day for learning new things."

I had to laugh, "Yes, it would seem that way."

CHAPTER 9

We all took several moments to recover. Michael was the first to stand up. When he spoke it was in a very hesitant manner, "It seems that creating life and shaping worlds may be only a small part of what we are capable of doing. I knew we could heal our creations, I am sure we have all done that from time to time but hurting each other, healing each other, perhaps destroying a brother. These are things I am not sure I ever wished to be capable of."

"It only stands to reason," Raphael stated, "There has to be a balance after all. All things must bow to that. One would look at a mountain and think that it would be impossible to harm it, yet water and wind slowly break it down. We have seen entire suns slowly fade and die. Nothing is truly indestructible."

Gabriel shook his head, "How can that be? We are energy and energy cannot be destroyed. Can it?"

Silence took hold of us again. We all stared blankly at each other, consumed with our own thoughts and philosophies until Uriel's gentle voice gained our attention.

"You are correct after a fashion Raphael, nothing is indestructible. Things shift, change, become different things. Look at a tree, it starts so small, then grows, becoming a home for some things, food for others, a respite for the sun for creatures that move about during the day. Eventually it dies, breaks down and becomes dirt again so other trees may grow from it. It has not truly been destroyed, it has merely become something else. Perhaps Remiel wasn't destroyed as such, he just returned to what we were before we became what we are now."

"Which is what?" Raguel, "If he became nothing and Remiel as we know him was gone, he was dead to us. Destroyed. Right?"

"In one way, yes," Uriel replied.

"You're making a rather fine distinction Uriel," Gabriel joined in, "If he had not come back, he would be gone, even if he had rejoined that which created us. I would not be able to speak with him. Just because parts of him still may exist somewhere within the greater energy, those parts are not Remiel."

I felt that I should be saying something since I was the one that had gone through the experience but I found that I had very little to add. It had all happened so fast, there was no way for me to know who or what I was at that moment.

"You wouldn't call a pile of dirt a tree," Seraqual started out, "I am not saying your statements are incorrect Uriel. You are looking at the broader view of things though and I think that undercuts the importance of what happened earlier. Whether or not Remiel rejoined the universal energy is beside the point, the Remiel we know would no longer be here. Which means we can be destroyed."

I decided that I should at least describe to them what had happened. I wasn't sure if Lucifer had and I felt that might be the only way I could add to the conversation, "I can tell you what I felt. I don't think it will give any answers or make anything easier to understand though." I told them everything, starting from Seraqual losing control up to when I returned and Lucifer had cradled me to him. When I finished their faces registered varying levels of horror, astonishment and concern. "This is why I put the new conditions on the agreement between Lucifer and Elohim, all of us were becoming too emotional."

"Uriel," Raphael spoke first, "I think you were correct in saying that he rejoined the universal energy and I disagree with Elohim's statement that we somehow pulled him back."

"Huh, statement?" Raquel said, "That was Elohim trying to make us fall for his arrogance and nothing else."

"Elohim is allowed to have his opinion," Michael stated.

Raguel chose not to reply. He didn't really have to, his eye roll and disdainful snort that followed Michael's words did it for him.

"We truly have no answers brothers," Gabriel interjected, "It is good for us to discuss these things and be more aware of the consequences of our choices. However, unless one of us wishes to be destroyed and hopefully come back again we won't know truly what happens or what it means."

Uriel rose and extended his hand to me, offering to help me stand, "Gabriel is right."

I took Uriel's hand and stood easily, I felt truly whole again.

Uriel continued, "For now we must watch over Elohim and Lucifer but not truly interfere unless one or the other breaks the agreement that Remiel created."

"That will take some doing," Seraqual pointed out, "They won't be too fond of us constantly checking on them and I am not too fond of delaying our tasks any more than we have already."

"Our tasks won't suffer from waiting a bit longer for us to get to them." Uriel surprised all of us with that statement. "The planets are patient, so is life itself. This situation is much more important. We, all of us, are in some way responsible for this issue and therefore we must resolve it."

"So what do you suggest?" Raphael asked.

I hadn't planned to say anything about Lillith and I'm still not sure what prompted me to speak, "I think all of you should spend some time with her."

Seraqual frowned at me, "Why?"

I looked at Uriel, he knew what was on my mind and gave me a slight nod. I sighed, "Lucifer has named her. Her name is Lillith. That is her name, not the name of her species."

They all spoke at once, except for Seraqual and Uriel, who already knew. "What?"

Michael's aura started to flicker and flash, silvery sparks shot from Raguel.

"Brothers..," I tried to calm them. Michael and Raguel closed their eyes and controlled themselves.

"Speak Remiel," Michael directed.

"We all know that he cares for her and we know that Elohim will not be satisfied quickly or swayed from his current path. It is obvious that Elohim believes he is correct and that we must all eventually conform with that belief. Neither these creations nor the contention between Elohim and Lucifer will be going away soon. I feel it is important that all of you know exactly how different of a creature Lillith is and her mate will be. She is like us in every way other than being able to hop between planets on a whim and create a living being from nothing. She thinks, she feels, she makes choices, she is not driven wholly by an instinct to hunt or mate. There is a reason Lucifer feels as he does, dismissing it as wrong or unbalanced will not change that."

Michael's green eyes pierced mine, searching for an explanation, "You have already spent time with her."

"Yes."

"And come to care for her in some way."

There was no point in denying it, "Yes."

"How will you be able to stay neutral then?" Michael asked. "Your judgment on this will be impaired because you allowed yourself to care."

Raphael, Gabriel and Seraqual were staring at me, they had agreed to follow my lead on this because they thought I was neutral, that I cared only for the balance. I was already regretting my lapse of truthfulness, then the thought hit me that I shouldn't have to.

"One of the reasons we have all been upset with the two of them is they kept things to themselves. I care about the balance, I always will. I just think that we should all be truthful and understand everything that is involved."

Raguel spoke, "I think Remiel is right."

That took me by surprise as he had threatened to destroy Lillith earlier.

"Why?" Raphael asked.

Raguel looked at each of us in turn before he spoke, "Because anything one of us creates, we are all responsible for. We have never sectioned off who did what. We have all created things on our own before, with little input from the others. When it comes down to it all of us are guardians of every thing from the largest animal to the tiniest grain of sand. Lillith and her kind are our responsibilities as well. We may not agree for the reason behind her being here but that is not the point. Each of us knows the intricacies of every single thing we have ever created, never once have we turned away from understanding a creation in the past. She is not at fault for existing and should not be punished for it. We need to separate her from our anger with our brothers."

That sentiment caused Michael to look away from us and start to pace, "Perhaps you are right, yet I am not sure I could do that. Her very existence is the problem."

"That may be," Uriel replied, "but that is not her fault. Remiel's idea has a few benefits that you are overlooking Michael. It will give us a reason to stay close to Lucifer whether he likes it or not and once Elohim understands that we are not being so blind to his plans as we were in the past perhaps he will moderate his ambitions and abandon this whole project."

They all looked at Uriel and even Seraqual appeared to be taking Uriel's words under serious consideration.

"As much as the idea of even being around her disgusts me," Seraqual stated, "you have a valid point Uriel. Fine. Let's get this over with. Either you or Remiel tell Lucifer what is going to happen. If we all show up he will just get angry."

Speaking further to Lucifer was the last thing I wanted to do at that moment. I needed some peace and quiet. "Uriel, would you? I need some time to myself, please."

"Of course. Get some peace brother, you have done more than enough to help us already."

Uriel embraced me again and when he released me Gabriel came up and did the same. One by one, all of them, even Michael wrapped their arms around me and it gave me hope that maybe things would work out for the best.

I left them then and ended up back on that same beach with the pink trees. Now that I was no longer having to head off conflicts, negotiate compromises or maintain a sense of decorum I found myself shaking, agitated and unable to calm down.

I had died, I had felt immense pain, I had attacked out of hate and rage. That feeling of being nothing came back to me again and almost brought me to my knees. I lost myself in the life around me, I let my form dissipate and one by one I flowed into every living thing I could find, grass, leaves, sea life, insects, the bright purple furred creature that survived off one tree and one tree only we had created here, rocks, water, all of it.

That moment, however brief, of feeling nothing haunted me, and it still does to this day. I had to reassure myself that I could still feel every particle of the world around me, sense every vibration, every ebb and flow of the lines of energy that connected the entirety of existence together. I lost myself in a molecule of sand, the symmetry, the perfection, how beautiful it was. A drop of water, with all it's fluidity, kept me entranced for an endless moment of time. When I had explored every millimeter of the planet I was on I shot to the skies and danced with the stars. I worked my way through the gases and stardust, spiraled and spun around black holes and suns. The immensity and perfection of the galaxy is matched only by the lack of flaws of its smallest part.

I heard my brothers calling to me from time to time. I sent back to them the sense that I was still alive but I was incapable of forming words or thoughts. All that mattered to me was being truly connected again, being alive. I have no real concept of how long I kept myself away from my brothers and my tasks. I went to so many places that I actually lost track of where I was. Time, location, tasks, they held little meaning for me until Raphael's emerald green ray of light appeared next to me.

"We've been looking for you," he said. "You made it quite challenging to keep up."

I hadn't taken a solid form often since leaving my brothers and that makes it slightly harder to pinpoint where we are.

"What is it? What do you need?" I can admit now that I was running, back then I didn't understand it. I was afraid, afraid of losing control, afraid of losing my family, afraid of the conflict that I knew was looming ahead of us all.

"Lillith's mate is completed. Lucifer would like you to be there and Lillith keeps asking if you are well."

I said nothing. Raphael floated next to me, suspended between the stars. His colors dimmed and stilled, I watched the planet below us slowly spin on its axis.

"Remiel, please."

"What has happened while I have been away?"

"Lucifer has been oddly cooperative. He didn't raise any large objections to us spending time with Lillith, who, although it bothers me to admit it, is a very endearing creature. He often left after he introduced us to her. She does have an endless stream of questions and observations about the world she lives in. Lucifer himself has become very withdrawn and quiet. Every time he has left her it seems more and more painful to the both of them."

I had feared as much. "And Elohim?"

"He's ignored us for the most part. Michael and Gabriel finally helped him on the design of her mate. He was getting more and more frustrated that he couldn't make Lillith's mate look anywhere close to her level of beauty. Raguel said we should just let him give up but Elohim prevailed on Michael. Gabriel pointed out that if a mate was not made for Lillith Lucifer may never leave that world and Elohim would be even more furious that Lillith was stolen from him."

"Her mate? What is he like?"

"Well he is not awakened yet but he looks decent enough."

"Did Elohim add his spark to her mate?" I hoped that my brothers had dissuaded Elohim from that path. If both of them were invested with extra energy I had no idea what type of dissonance that would cause.

"He apparently chose not to. Gabriel thinks it is because he does not want his creation to be that strong. Elohim has not spent any time with Lillith but I am sure Michael and Gabriel described her to him."

"Why does Lucifer want me there?" I felt Gabriel's discomfort at the question before he answered.

"Lucifer wants you to stand in his stead when Elohim presents her mate to her. He told Uriel that he could not promise to control himself if he was there for it. He will not admit his feelings for her are wrong but at least he's admitting that they affect him."

Frustration surged through me, "Why am I always getting put between these two?" I snarled. I wasn't entirely surprised at the request I was just angered that Lucifer was refusing to see this through. A small part of me thought it was cruel of him to not be there when Lillith was finally exposed to the reality of her situation. I debated on confronting him about it but stopped myself. He was keeping his word and trying to make this as non confrontational as possible and I shouldn't scold him for that.

"Fine. I'll go to them." I searched through space and time, found Lucifer and sent myself to him.

"Remiel!" Lillith shouted with joy when I appeared. I had not been prepared for that. She dropped Lucifer's hand, ran to me and placed her arms around me. "We have missed you! You've been gone so long!"

97

I looked over her head at Lucifer, such pain was in his bearing. A small smile graced his features but his shoulders were pulled forward as he stood and there was hardly any joy left in his eyes. "Thank you," his subdued voice entered my mind.

"Oh Lucifer, why?" I replied.

"I can not stop what I feel Remiel but I have to keep my word to you."

I looked away from him and into Lillith's face. She was so thrilled to see me. Once again her personality and energy captured my attention. "I have missed you too Lillith. Thank you for the warm greeting."

"I have met all of you now, except Elohim," she told me, "and learned so many things! Lucifer says my mate is ready too. I hope he is like all of you."

She gripped me tightly once more then returned to Lucifer's side.

"I hope so too." I wasn't sure what to say next since I had no idea if Lucifer had told her I was to take her to see her mate. His golden eyes closed tightly as he wrapped his arm around her shoulders. He hadn't told her yet. I found myself wishing I did not have to bear witness to this moment.

He gently placed his free hand on her cheek, "Lillith, look at me."

"Yes Lucifer?"

"I..." he froze, unable to speak. I shifted my perceptions to view the energies around them and had to stop myself from starting yet another fight with Lucifer. There was hardly any separation between them, Lucifer's aura and colors swirled around and through Lillith's and she through him. Even though, according to my brothers, he had tried to keep himself separate from her they had somehow become so entwined as to almost be a single being.

Human often speak of soul mates, of just "knowing" when they have met that one person that completes them. Lucifer had voluntarily given part of his very essence to Lillith and it had

98

grown within her, binding the two of them at the very core of who they were. I don't think I truly understood what the cost of that would be until that moment. Even if Lillith chose to stay with her mate, Lucifer would pine for her and she for him. Nothing could change that now.

"Do you want me to tell her?" I whispered to his mind.

"No, I must do this."

"What is it?" Lillith asked, "You seem so sad." She didn't understand what this separation would truly mean, not yet.

"Remiel is going to take you to your mate," he finally spoke, "I have a task to do."

Something about him or his words triggered something in her, the smile left her face. She tilted her head against his hand, placing her hand gently over his. "Will you be back soon?"

He pulled her close, "I am not sure," he whispered, "Remiel will watch over you." Then he briefly placed his lips on top of her head and left us.

"Lucifer!" She looked at me, panic in her eyes, "Remiel? He has never said that before. He always says he will return soon. What is wrong? He seemed so upset."

What to tell her? If I told her how much he cared for her would that prejudice her choice? I tried for somewhere between the truth and a lie, "He is sad because he had to leave when something so important is about to happen. He would much rather be here with you. I think Lucifer also knows once you meet your mate that the two of you should have time to get to know each other. He will miss you very much."

The panic on her face slowly changed to sadness. "But, I do not want him to miss me. I do not want to miss him either." She looked up at the sky, "Lucifer! Please do not be gone for too long! Please!"

My heart twisted at her plea.

99

"Protect her from him brother, please." Lucifer's voice filled my mind, almost blinding me with its feelings of love for her.

I reached out, pulled her close to me and found I had no words for either of them.

CHAPTER 10

We stayed like that for a few moments then I pulled away from her. "I will find out where Elohim is and take us to him." I hoped he wasn't too far. I was hesitant to transport Lillith as Lucifer had, one of us being bound to her in any way was one too many.

I sent my thought out, "Elohim? I am with Lillith and she is ready to meet her mate."

"Remiel? So you have returned." He didn't seem all that pleased to hear from me.

"Yes." He was only a few miles away. "Lillith and I will walk to you and meet you shortly."

"Is Lucifer not coming?" I could tell by his tone that he had been looking forward to watching Lucifer's reaction.

"No, he had something to attend to. We will see you soon." I chose to not dwell on Elohim's desires to upset Lucifer further. Lillith's hand was still in mine and we started walking.

She held my hand much tighter than she ever had before. I wanted to offer her some sort of comfort but anything I thought of seemed trite. I had no real idea how she and her mate would get along, it's not something we had ever had to worry about before. Then there was the issue of Elohim, it bothered me that he had ignored the majority of us while I had been away. It was just another sign of his arrogance in my opinion. We continued to walk without speaking for quite some time.

"Are we getting closer?" She asked in a timid voice.

"Yes. Do you need to rest?"

"No, I.." She stopped walking and looked at me, tears started drifting down her cheeks. "He's left me. He won't be back will he? It's because we are different, we are not supposed to be with each other. Your brothers, they all seemed very," she paused searching for the right word.

"Upset? Nervous? Guarded?" I tried to help.

"Guarded. Yes, thank you Remiel. They did not seem as friendly as you or Lucifer. They spoke with me, answered my questions but did not seem to be happy to do so. Raguel, Uriel and Gabriel were not as guarded but Michael did not stay long. Raphael and Seraqual were all right I guess." Her eyes shifted away from mine and I couldn't quite define the expression on her face, "I am different, from everything else you have created, aren't I?"

I had forgotten just how perceptive she was. "Yes, you are."

She tucked her lower lip under her teeth, chewing on it in an oddly adorable gesture. "Did Lucifer do something wrong, spending so much time with me? Is that why he is so sad now? Is that why he had to leave?"

I decided that if she was capable of the thought process to ask the questions and make the connections than she was worthy of an explanation. "Yes and no," I sighed. "Let's sit a moment, this will take some time to explain."

I told her how Elohim wanted a creation that would show him respect and how Lucifer had added his some of his own spark to her because he felt that her kind should be seen as equals, not as something that should see us as something beyond them. I phrased everything in as neutral of a fashion as I could, I didn't want to prejudice her against her mate or Elohim. That would break the agreement Elohim, Lucifer and I had made. When I finished she looked at me very several long moments. As I spoke her face displayed so many emotions. Lillith hadn't learned how to hide her feelings and they were all on display for me to see, astonishment, confusion, concern and deepening understanding all kept pace with my words. Her eyes would widen, wrinkles and creases would appear on her face in various places, she would chew her lower lip, her eyes would shift from side to side. No other animal we created before her had such a mobile face that could show many things. Yet again my breath was taken away by watching her and I found myself agreeing with Lucifer that everything we had learned up until that moment had been captured in Lillith's design.

What she said after several moments of taking it all in shook me to my very core. "What if I told Elohim thank you for creating me? Would that make him less mad at Lucifer? Could he come back then? If Elohim is the one that truly brought me to life I should respect him. Lucifer may have gifted me with so much but without Elohim I would be nothing."

In all our considerations we never once thought about how she may view things and she was right. Whether or not I agreed with Elohim's desire to have a creation that worshiped him, without his gift the rest of us were rather useless. She had seen to the core of the matter in a matter of minutes and had come up with a possible solution to the whole dilemma. Lucifer could not fault her for her decision or feelings on the matter, she had come up with them on her own and that was the whole point of this.

"I think Elohim would very much appreciate you thanking him, and yes, I believe that would help calm the waters between he and Lucifer."

A triumphant grin appeared on her face, washing away all her prior concerns. "Then that is what I will do, and thank him for making my mate as well." She stood up, took hold of my hand and we resumed our walk.

We crested a gentle, grassy hill that overlooked a small river that ran through shallow, flower covered meadow. Red, pink, blue and yellow blossoms were scattered about. Birds were hopping and dancing around them, splitting their time between eating and courting each other. I felt Elohim reach out to my brothers and shafts of silver, gold, green, blue and brown appeared around him and became still for a moment. Between one blink of an eye and the next they took their forms and turned to watch Lillith and I join them.

I felt something behind us, Lucifer. I took a quick look over my shoulder but nothing was there. I made my thought very soft and targeted to keep the others from overhearing, "Lucifer?" He failed to reply but I knew he was watching. All I could do was hope for the best and that he would keep his word and not cause another fight.

It appeared that between the time when Raphael found me and now, Elohim had awakened Lillith's mate. Elohim had placed her mate in front of him and was resting a slightly glowing hand on his shoulder. I saw evidence of Michael's work which is always rather rough hewn compared to the rest of us. Her mate stood a few inches taller than her, was broad shouldered, a shade or two darker than she was with hair the color of night and brown eyes. His hair stopped at his shoulders whereas hers reached half way down her back, his features were symmetrical but not nearly as polished and shapely as Lillith's. Her face was filled with gently sloping lines and soft angles; his was more angular yet less defined and felt unfinished to me.

Lillith hesitated when she saw both her mate and Elohim standing in front of her. "Take your time," I told her. She responded with a slight head shake, then she released my hand and walked directly up to both of them.

"Hello Elohim, I am Lillith. Thank you for bringing me to life and creating this mate for me."

All of us, including Elohim, were completely speechless. She reached her right hand out and touched her mate's arm. He flinched slightly, then slowly raised his hand to copy her gesture.

"That's right," she encouraged, "Now watch." She took his hand, placed it over hers and opened and closed her fist, just as Lucifer had done when she first awakened. It took him slightly longer to understand than it her but soon he was repeating her movements. She smiled at him, "Perfect!"

The corners of his mouth hesitantly curled up, it looked a bit like he was baring his teeth at her but he had just been awakened so the emotions behind the movement were not there yet. That spark and force of life that Lillith had when she came to life was obviously missing in her mate. Lucifer's gift had given her so much more than we realized at first.

"Have you given him a name?" She boldly asked Elohim.

By now most of us had recovered from her greeting, Elohim's face was conflicted. When she had first thanked him, a surprised yet smug, condescending smile had taken hold. As she took charge of teaching her mate in the exact same way Lucifer had taught her, his smile had quickly turned twisted and dark.

"His name is Adam," he answered, barely keeping his tone in check. "I will be teaching you from now on."

My brothers all looked sharply at him. I stepped closer to Lillith and sent my thought to him, "That was not the terms of the agreement." I did not want to verbalize our disagreement just yet. Not with Lillith standing in harm's way.

Before he could respond to me Lillith spoke up again, "Remiel told me about how all of you were upset that Lucifer spent so much time with me and how you are in charge of keeping the balance. He also said that Lucifer gifted me with something extra, his spark, without telling you."

All eyes shifted to me, the looks ranged from accusatory to disbelief.

"What he gifted me with," she continued, "It made me different from what you had intended. While I thank him for that gift and the time he spent with me, what he gave me would be pointless without your gift of life Elohim. Lucifer is hurting now because of what happened, he and Remiel fought and all of you were upset. I do not want Lucifer, or any of you, to be more upset because of me, or us." She gestured to Adam. "I will teach him. You have all taught me so many things already and I know you have so many tasks elsewhere. You need not take any more time away from them to teach us."

She disengaged Adam's hand from hers, took two more steps

105

forward and embraced Elohim, who merely stood there, utter confusion on his face. "Thank you again. We owe you our lives." She released him, took hold of Adam's hand and looked at all of us, excitement in her eyes and a sweet smile on her face, "Thank you for answering all my of questions when you came to meet me. I will make sure to show Adam everything you showed me."

As soon as she finished speaking she turned and started to walk upstream, Adam hesitated, confused. She gave him another smile and tugged lightly on his hand. He looked at Elohim who waved his hand in the direction Lillith was headed. Adam cocked his head to one side and took a few shaky steps.

"Oh, I am sorry," Lillith said, "I thought you had walked already. Here, I'll help you." She placed his arm around her shoulders and steadied him as they moved farther away from us. By the time they had gotten about thirty feet away Adam's arm had moved from her shoulders to her waist as she pointed to various things and explained what they were.

Raguel rubbed his hands together, a pleased smile on his face, "Well, that solves that problem. She said thank you, acknowledged that you brought her to life and has her mate. We're done here now, right?"

Elohim's mouth kept opening and closing, his eyes were filled with anger but Lillith had outmaneuvered him. She was truly Lucifer's equal in that aspect. Between the extra conditions I had placed on the agreement and Lillith's actions he had no room to protest or demand something else.

Uriel and Raphael had their hands covering their mouths but their shoulders were twitching from their attempts to control their laughter, even Michael was smiling. Gabriel and Seraqual had both let out large sighs of relief. Suddenly Uriel's face went blank as something behind me attracted his attention. I turned around and had to squint my eyes against the brilliance of Lucifer's flaring aura. We all held our collective breath.

"Don't push it," Raguel snarled under his breath.

Lucifer stood on the top of the hill; his aura battling the sun itself for intensity and power, a smile filled with pride and joy on his face. The full extent of his old arrogance and confidence was back in his eyes and bearing. He said nothing as he stared at Elohim.

"You dare?" Elohim whispered.

Lucifer's eyes shifted to me and his chin dipped in a slight nod. A salute and a reminder that he had kept his word. Multiple shades of reds and purples danced around him but were soon taken over by the pure white light that started from his head and flowed down his arms and back encompassing his torso and shooting out on either side of him. The white light reached up above his shoulders and head as his grin grew even broader. Suddenly his aura froze and the edges of the blazing white light that was behind him slowly turned purple and red. The colors flexed and shifted, like wings made of pure energy, and he disappeared.

I looked back at Elohim, flames of power rose from him but he said nothing. He looked at each of us in turn, then in the direction Lillith and Adam had gone. The ground beneath me started to shake and the skies started to darken.

"Elohim!" Uriel commanded, "Enough! You have no grounds for this. Lucifer kept his word. Lillith accepted your mate. What else do you want?"

Elohim's hands balled into fists and his face became distorted with darkness and hate. He took a step towards Uriel then Michael appeared in front of him and spoke, emphasizing each word he said "The agreement was kept, brother. You agreed to this, keep your word as Lucifer did." Michael's aura surrounded him, solidifying in a way we had never seen before. Bronze and gold shimmering armor covered him completely, concealing his entire body. That seemed to get Elohim's attention, he stepped away from Michael and the flames flickered and disappeared.

"Fine," He ground out between his lips before turning away and disappearing as well.

Michael's appearance returned to normal, a small smile caused his lips to twitch. "She has Lucifer's confidence."

"Indeed," Uriel agreed. "And his skill with words."

"His face when she embraced him," Seraqual said with a slight chuckle.

It started with Raphael who joined in with Seraqual's chuckling, then spread to Gabriel and Uriel. Once Uriel started laughing I couldn't help myself. Lillith may not be a divine being but she had managed to catch all nine of us off guard, it was too much really and we erupted into laughter.

CHAPTER 11

Things went along quietly for quite some time after that. We all dispersed and returned to our tasks. Despite Lucifer's show that he put on after Lillith's acceptance of her mate he never really recovered his former joy about things. He completed what he had to but his creations lacked that extra bit of perfection that had always been his hallmark before. He rarely spoke to any of us and seemed to be completely avoiding me.

Gabriel and I were caught up in devising creatures that could survive in a truly harsh environment that went from sub freezing temperatures to scalding and back again in a two day long cycle on a world far away from where Lillith and Adam reside. We were somewhat stumped when Gabriel decided to broach the topic of Lucifer's depression.

"Has he spoken to you yet?" Gabriel asked.

I was distracted by the task at hand and didn't understand at first, "Who?"

"Lucifer."

"No," I sighed, "I have been trying to give him time to come to terms with what happened but I am not sure if that's the best way to handle this anymore. He seems to be getting worse. Uriel said that when they were working together recently that Lucifer refused to speak about anything other than the task they were doing. Elohim seems to be handling things better but I sense some sort of deception there. He and Michael have become inseparable which bothers me. Seraqual mentioned to me that Elohim has become rather dismissive of he and Raguel as well."

"Yes, Raphael mentioned that to me as well." Gabriel replied, "Perhaps you should go to him Remiel. Raphael and I have tried to get Lucifer to confide in us but he refuses to. Raguel has made a point of trying to stay near him but Lucifer finally made it clear that he did not need to be watched over. I have checked in on

Lillith and Adam..."

"You have?" I interrupted. I was surprised that he had done that. I had as well but had not mentioned it to anyone.

"Yes, they seem to be doing fine but when she is alone she tends to look up into the sky and speak his name." He looked away from me as his aura shifted restlessly. "She misses him."

"I know. I have seen this as well. The agreement cannot be changed though. It would just put us right back where we were."

When his gaze fixed upon me again the amount of guilt and pain that haunted his face took me by surprise, "What's wrong brother?"

"Michael and I, we should have paid much more attention to what Elohim was thinking and how obsessed he had become. I feel as if we could have stopped this or at least made it much less divisive. We would have given him a docile creation and not pushed the boundaries like Lucifer did. Perhaps Elohim would have grown tired of trying to create something so complex. Honestly Remiel, without Lucifer's help Elohim would have struggled to complete her. Even with Michael's help Adam is not nearly as refined as Lillith. We should have humored Elohim and kept an eye on him. We..." he trailed off into silence and looked off into the distance.

"It is not entirely your fault Gabriel." I tried to comfort him.

"Perhaps not but it feels as if it is. I rushed to condemn Lucifer for doing that which I chose to dismiss. I was condemning him with my words but in my mind I was condemning myself. Look how this has hurt them. Lucifer may never recover, who knows what Elohim is really thinking and Lillith longs for the one being she should never have been allowed to have feelings for in the first place. It will never be as it was, we will never truly be a family again."

I saw an opportunity in Gabriel's words. As far as I knew no one had really apologized to Lucifer for attacking him in the days following Lillith's awakening. I'll be the first to admit that how he had handled the situation was lacking a large amount of tact or even concern for the rest of us, but as Gabriel pointed out, all the rest of us had failed to learn the depth of Elohim's obsession. If any of us had said yes to helping Elohim, Lillith, if she had even had been created at all, would be a much different creature and Elohim and Lucifer's immense arrogance driven personalities would not have had a direct confrontation.

"Things may never be exactly the way they were, " I started out, "but they do not have to get worse either. Many of you were rather harsh on Lucifer. Believe me when I tell you that he regrets the discord that his actions brought." I was hoping Gabriel would volunteer to apologize to Lucifer as Lucifer had apologized to me.

Gabriel's face hardened, "What he did was wrong Remiel."

"No one is denying that, but he is not the only one at fault."

I watched him struggle with it for several minutes. You have to understand, the balance, the need to keep it, it has always been paramount to all of us and Lucifer's solution to Elohim's madness went against the very core of what we are. Giving Lillith some of his divinity, he had to know deep down that it would only make things worse. When I left after our fight I had come to terms with the fact that his betrayal of the balance was truly what had driven me to attack him, not the manipulation of us all, but his willingness to push the boundaries so far without any thought to the consequences of his choices.

Gabriel's aura stilled finally, the confusion in his face cleared and he gazed at me with resolution in his eyes. "You are right. I shouldn't condemn Lucifer for being who he is, none of us should. None of us are perfect, we all bear some of the blame for the way things are now. Once we finish here I will talk to him, I just hope he listens and it helps."

I gave him a brief smile and we resumed our task. True to his word, several days later when we had finished he left to speak with Lucifer who was with Uriel again.

"Remiel?" Uriel's voice came to me soon after Gabriel had left me.

"Yes?"

"Gabriel is here and is speaking with Lucifer who, surprisingly, is actually listening. I thought you should know. I assume you had some small part in convincing him to speak with Lucifer."

I had to chuckle, Uriel knew me all too well. "A very small part. Is it going well?"

"Lucifer seems somewhat stunned with what Gabriel is saying..wait a moment."

I'll admit I waited with bated breath for Uriel to speak again. Any improvement in how my brothers were acting towards each other, no matter how small, was something that I was desperately hoping for. I love all my brothers, even now, after all that has happened. There are things between us that no human could understand, our responsibility as creators and immortality, they are an immense burden to bear alone.

"Well done. Lucifer embraced Gabriel and seems to be thanking him for whatever he said. Gabriel appears very relieved and grateful. Oh, that's nice to see."

"What is?" I could sense Uriel's joy and relief at something.

"Gabriel left but Lucifer just turned to me and smiled. Not his usual arrogant smile but something much different, more innocent. He has been very somber since he last saw Lillith. Gabriel forgave him, is that correct?"

Some of the tension and distress I had been feeling dissipated at Uriel's words. "After a fashion." I relayed Gabriel's and my conversation to him.

"It's a start," Uriel replied. He was much more excited and pleased than his words would lead one to believe. I could feel it. "I have been purposely keeping Lucifer with me more than usual to keep an eye on him for several reasons. I sent Michael to keep an eye on Elohim."

"Ah, I was wondering why they had become so much closer."

"It pains me to say it," he continued, "But I found myself not trusting either of them to keep their word in full. I felt that I should get ahead of any possible future issues instead of letting them catch us unawares again. So far they have both been true the agreement though as far as we can tell."

"Good."

"Yes. Now if Gabriel can convince some of the others to speak to Lucifer we may get him back to something close to his old self. It has been hard to see him like this. As much as we may have all wished he were given less to grandiose displays and perfectionist ways I find that I miss it."

I remembered all the beautiful, heart stopping things Lucifer had created over the years, how truly empty many of the worlds would be without his sheer genius and talent. The way my brothers had been describing his recent creations now troubled me greatly. He had never created anything that was dull, imperfect or without gifting it with something truly unique before. It appeared that was all he was turning out now.

"I think the universe itself misses it," I replied. "I am glad I could help in some way. Thank you for letting me know what happened."

"Of course," Uriel answered, "I will keep you informed if any of the others appear as well."

For the first time since Lillith awakened I found I had a small bit of hope.

Several days later Lucifer appeared next to me as I stood on a hill above a river I was cutting into the surface of yet another planet. His appearance startled me so much I lost focus on what I was doing and the river double backed on itself and started running upstream right next to where it was running downstream. I

113

remember stopping myself from frowning at him or saying anything harsh, fixing the river and turning to face him. I wasn't upset that he had made me lose focus, I was more irritated at myself for the slight error.

"I rather liked it the other way brother," he said with a small grin on his face. It was heartening to hear him making fun of my errors.

"Well in that case, I shall put it back," I replied. "It's good to see you."

He smiled again, it didn't quite reach into his eyes, there was shame there still. "I wanted to thank you Remiel, for talking to Gabriel." He lowered his eyes to stare at the ground in front of my feet, something he had never, ever done in the past. "I should have gone to him, to all of them to try to resolve things in a better fashion."

He was skirting around it but I knew that he, in his own way, was accepting responsibility for what had happened. "I just felt.."

I waited for him to resume speaking.

"Well, I felt that they would not accept anything I had to say. I have thought quite extensively about everything that happened. I will not say that I would not have fought for Lillith and her kind to still be independent and strong, but I may have taken a different path to assure it if I were in the same position again."

He raised his eyes to mine again, there was more that he needed to say.

"What I gifted her with, it binds me to her in ways that I never thought possible. She says my name and I feel it, I hear it. I feel her sadness. It is so hard not to go to her but my promise to you, to my brothers, is much more important to me." He paused again, when he resumed speaking his voice was choked with such emotion, such love, "She will eventually pass on, as all our creations do." Once he finished speaking he looked away but I saw the tears in his golden eyes.

114

I found I had no words for him, this was yet another thing that none of us ever expected. It had always been so easy for us to reach out to one another and provide comfort when needed that the idea of not being able to go to someone I loved who was suffering struck me so deeply. I began to understand that Lucifer's depression was not just his, it was hers as well. Words would not help so I placed my arm around his shoulders.

"May I see?" I wanted to truly understand what he was feeling. I could sense some of it already but I knew it wasn't the true depth of it.

His shoulders tightened under my arm, "You will not be pleased with what you see. The bonds between her and I have grown even though I have stayed as far from her as possible. I am not sure how or why, but you must believe me that I have not visited her or had any contact with her since she took Adam as her mate."

If I had any doubt as to the truthfulness of his words, it was banished when he looked at me again. The Lucifer I had known since the beginning of time was gone, who stood before me at that moment was someone in the grips of immense loss and pain begging for me to believe him and find it within myself to trust him.

"Beloved brother. I stood by you before, I will continue to do so. I promise."

He lowered his gaze again, "Thank you. Go ahead, look."

The moment I reached out to him I was overwhelmed with the chaos that took hold of me. "Lucifer! What it this?" I was so disoriented that I had no idea where to begin to unravel it all.

"That is Lillith and I, we no longer have a beginning or end. Look at the lines of energy first, it will help."

I did as he suggested and was even more astounded. He had somehow managed to separate and cushion her line of energy from the flow of the universe, limiting it's disruptive nature but the cost to him was immense. They had truly become mated on the deepest level possible and I had no idea if they could ever be split apart again.

"What? How? Why?"

He sighed. "Go deeper, brother. You've barely scratched the surface. I'll explain as much as I can when you are done."

I found myself wondering if by looking I was going to somehow get pulled into the chaos that had once been my brother. I proceeded with much trepidation and realized that the reason Lucifer's creations as of late had been so subpar was because he'd been involved in something much more complicated. He had found a way to conceal his state from the rest of us along with limiting the amount of damage this unnatural bond between he and Lillith could cause while being awash in the intensity of her emotions along with his.

Our emotional range up until this point had been fairly limited, mainly because everything had been so harmonious between us. Even with what I had felt from my brothers and my own recent anger I was in no way prepared for the aching sense of loss, of loneliness, of soul deep pain that I felt from both he and Lillith. I started trying to sort through things by meticulously searching for what I knew Lucifer felt like, homing in on that and then trying to comprehend the rest. Once I separated Lucifer out I allowed myself to touch Lillith's threads. Her emotions were so violent compared to ours, when she felt joy, she felt it so intensely, same with fear, pain, anger, confusion and her moods were in a constant state of flux. It was a wonder that Lucifer hadn't gone entirely mad by this point.

A soft whisper came to me, "Lucifer? I miss you. Please come back."

Since I was connected to both her and him at that moment I was able to witness the true nature of their connection. As her words reached him, so did her sense of loss, of confusion as to why he had been away so long. I felt him shudder and heard him gasp at the intensity of it and he tried to stop any sense of himself from going back to her but he couldn't. A small strand of black tinted lavender left him, traveling down the lines of energy back to her.

"I know you hear me, I can feel you," she said. "I am sure you are doing what is best. I....," she stopped speaking but words were not really necessary. What she felt, he felt. She had wanted to say that she loved him but perhaps something told her she shouldn't.

I withdrew from him, closing my eyes as I tried to process what I had seen. When I opened them again I saw that he was waiting for me to erupt into anger and accuse him of an even further betrayal but I felt none of those things. What I felt was an overwhelming desire to ease his pain. "Explain everything to me," I told him, "You cannot keep this up on your own. Allow me to help."

CHAPTER 12

"No Remiel, I cannot allow that. That would only make things worse, more out of balance. It's complicated enough as it is. Thank you though." He collected himself, composed his features and continued, "From what I have been able to discern, the spark I gave her will stay connected to me for as long as she lives. It also creates an open line of communication between her and I similar to how all of us speak to each other. She seems to draw strength from me when she is upset. I appear to get some back when I become troubled but it is not the same type of energy as what she pulls from me. I have been working on trying to find a way to minimize the amount and affect it has on me but so far I have not had much success."

"How much is this weakening you?"

He shrugged and his left eyebrow arched, "I am not sure. My tasks have suffered as of late more because of the amount of time I have spent trying to make sense of all this more than actual weakness."

"You have managed to conceal this somehow. As bound together as you are now I should be able to feel it much more than I am. The fact that Seraqual has not had another breakdown is also testament to that. How?"

A hint of the old Lucifer came back into his eyes, his aura shifted to a vibrant shade of purple and rippled briefly around him. "Skill, pure skill."

Prior to Lillith I would have been irritated at his words, yet this time they made me smile. I had missed him too. "Would it be too much to ask you to elaborate?"

"Look again at the lines," he requested. When I did I was stunned, nothing like the chaos that I had seen earlier was evident in the world around me. I saw his line, entwined with hers as I had seen earlier when Seraqual had pointed it out but it looked like that was the full extent of the distortion. There was no real hint as to the depth of it, how she was able to take energy from him, the shared emotions they were feeling. I looked closer, "You are using lines from the plants and animals to mask it. How?" Every living thing has a connection to everything else, Lucifer had devised a way to make the connection between he and Lillith look like something else entirely.

"I am not shifting them, fear not, I am not creating more chaos, I promise. I discovered that I could create an image of those lines and drape it over ours. It is challenging as I have to constantly take into account what is around me and make sure it matches well enough. The image seems to mute out the reverberation of the distortion that even Seraqual's acuteness is fooled well enough. This has been one of the main reasons I have been keeping my distance from all of you recently. I had to.."

I had managed to process, at least in part, what I had seen when it hit me, "You had to hide this, lie to us again. Correct? Have you truly learned nothing?"

Red tinged flashes appeared, he closed his eyes and looked away. "No, that is not what I am doing. How could I tell you what was wrong without knowing the full extent of the situation?"

"Lucifer. You make it much harder to believe those words when you have put such effort into hiding the problem."

"I.." he stopped speaking, terror took hold of his features, his arm shot out like he was trying to catch something, "Lillith!"

"What's wrong?"

"She's falling into the canyon!"

He started to shift to save her when I stopped him, "No! You stay here. The agreement must hold. I'll go." I shifted before he could argue with me about it, followed her line and caught her just before she hit the raging river.

"Remiel!" She screamed when I appeared and stopped her

downward momentum.

At that moment I knew that I, like Lucifer, cared far too much for her. I no longer saw her as a just creation of ours that once brought to life we allowed to live whatever life it could. She had become something akin to family to me, which made me culpable in destroying the balance. It pains me to admit it but I considered letting her fall. She would hardly be the first animal to fall into a river and drown and her death would solve so many things. Then I looked into her face.

She placed her arms around my neck, "Thank you! Thank you!" She held on so tight it is probably a good thing I don't actually require oxygen. She shook as I held her, her eyes wide with relief and a few tears slid down her cheeks. So vulnerable, so innocent and trusting. I could no more fail her than I could my brothers.

"I have her," I sent to Lucifer, then spoke to her. "Are you harmed?"

"No."

We were hovering over the river, I looked up and saw Adam standing on the edge of the canyon looking down. I started drifting up towards where he was standing and he fearfully backed away. "What happened?" I asked Lillith as we rose.

Her usually open and honest face became clouded and she averted her eyes from mine. "I fell. I was collecting some plants on the edge and the ground moved underneath me."

Admittedly my brothers and I had only recently started to lie to each other but I knew what the signs were. For Lillith, who was still so new, to feel that she should hide something from me was worrisome. I halted our ascent. "That's all that happened? You slipped?"

She shifted nervously in my arms. "Yes Remiel."

I certainly wouldn't force her to talk. I resumed our progress and once we got to the top set her on her feet.

120

Adam was standing several feet away and he refused to look at us. "Please, please, do not be angry with me wise one. Please," he stammered. "She refuses to listen to what I say and thinks that what you tell me is false."

I had absolutely no idea what he was talking about and looked at Lillith.

"Adam," her tone was harsh and filled with frustration, "This is Remiel, not the one that you say talks to you. I keep telling you there are several of them and now you know the truth."

Adam's brought his eyes up to look at her, his lips curled in disgust but there was fear in his eyes, "Quiet! You will anger him. If this one is not who speaks to me than he is the enemy and you should have nothing to do with him. I have told you how they betrayed him, the one who made us."

I was speechless. It took me several moments to come up with even the simplest thing to say, "Adam, I am Remiel and am hardly your enemy, nor did I betray anyone. Who is this that speaks to you?" I already knew but I had to keep speaking to try to calm my quickly rising anger. "How does he speak to you?"

Adam remained silent and turned away from me, Lillith answered for him. "Adam says he speaks to him in dreams and other ways as well. He just calls himself our creator. I told him that Lucifer and Elohim both created us.."

"Do not speak that name!" Adam shouted.

"Which name?" I asked.

Lillith wrapped her arms around her chest, dropped her eyes away from me and hunched her shoulders forward. "Lucifer. Adam says our creator says Lucifer is evil and not to be trusted."

Lavender colored the air around me, I felt the ground start to tremble under my feet and Lillith slowly backed away, Adam turned and ran. "Remiel? Oh no, I upset you."

I stared at her, then looked down at my hands which were fully enveloped in shimmering balls of lavender and white power. "Uriel! Come now!" I projected my thought so strongly I felt him wince in pain when it hit him, "Gabriel! Come! You!" I pointed at Lillith, "Tell my brothers what you just told me."

Uriel and Gabriel manifested on either side of me, "Remiel? What is wrong?" Uriel asked.

"Listen to Lillith," I snarled in return. She repeated what she had said.

Uriel became engulfed in such intense dark green light it came close to mirroring the dark of night, making it seem like his blue eyes were hovering within a roiling thunderstorm. His aura crashed into mine creating a thunderous sound. I looked at Gabriel who 's body was barely visible within a burning blue flame.

"How dare he?" Gabriel whispered. "To say that we have betrayed him and Lucifer is evil."

We looked at each other, nodded, found Elohim and shifted.

Uriel barely beat us there. Elohim was sitting atop a mountain working on something that looked like a creation similar to Adam and Lillith, something was different about it but I was too angered to pay much attention. Uriel crashed into Elohim, knocking him to the ground and they rolled off the side.

"What is the meaning of this?" Elohim shouted as they tumbled down the mountain.

"We betrayed you?" Uriel growled as lighting crashed into the granite around them, "You have gone beyond arrogance into insanity Elohim."

Elohim began to laugh then he shifted, disappeared from underneath Uriel, reappeared above him and drove his hand into Uriel's back, Uriel screamed in pain. Elohim's hand changed into a shaft of fiery power and drove deeper into Uriel.

"Uriel!" Gabriel cried as he raised his hand and called down ice blue lighting that struck Elohim, throwing him back several feet. I resorted to a different tactic and pointed my hand at the earth beneath Elohim, wrenching it asunder while hurling my own power at him which knocked him into the quickly widening gully. I started to pull the earth back together in hopes of temporarily trapping Elohim but flames shot up above the earth. He hovered above us for a moment, flickered and reappeared next to the thing he had been working on. "Awaken and serve me," he said. The unnatural pull on the energies around us knocked me down. The creation arose, it had wings and glowed with an energy it should never have possessed.

"What would you have me do Father?" It asked, it's voice monotone and obedient. There was no independent thought in it's eyes.

"Protect me," Elohim ordered then vanished.

This new creation came hurtling at us and chose to attack me first. It's hand struck my face sending me backwards several feet. I wrapped my will around it's body and began to crush it. It struggled against me.

"Remiel, wait," Uriel said, his voice filled with pain. "We need to find out what this is."

"Just another abomination that Elohim seeks to control," I replied. "He accuses us of betrayal then does this. I have reached my limit of understanding." And in an act that I regret to this day I used my will, the power that the universe had gifted me with to create life and ripped this winged creation apart from the inside out. I did not merely crush it, I reduced it back to the dust and ash that Elohim had used to build it. It cried out in pain, screaming Father over and over again until there was not enough of it's structure left to create sound. Uriel and Gabriel stared at me in horror and fear.

Gabriel stepped away from me, "What have you done?"

"I have made a choice. Elohim has turned his back on us. Lucifer

123

has kept his word, even though it is destroying him. I will no longer pretend that Elohim cares about the balance, our tasks or anything other than his obsession to be worshiped. What we must do now is try to limit the damage Elohim can do. If that means destroying every perverted and unbalanced thing he makes, so be it."

"Including Adam and Lillith?" Gabriel's words made me pause.

I was about to respond when Uriel's eyes closed and for a brief moment I felt my connection to him weaken. I rushed to him, "Brother?"

"I just need a few moments," he murmured.

I changed into my true form and rose over him, "Let me help." I found that I did not have to think about how to aid him, I just did it. Whatever injury Elohim inflicted upon him called to me and my will, my energy rushed in to repair it. It was as if his injuries were mine and I knew exactly what was needed.

Once Uriel was healed I resumed my walking about form and looked at Gabriel. "Lillith and Adam are not direct threats to us. Whatever this most recent creation he made was. It was different, somehow he made it something even closer to us than they are. It possessed an energy like ours but it wasn't his personal spark."

"Remiel," Uriel spoke, "You said that Lucifer has kept his word even though it is destroying him. Explain."

"No, he will. I have had my fill of being in the middle of all of this." I sent my thought out. "Lucifer, join us immediately please. You will tell Uriel and Gabriel what you told me and we have some things to tell you. I am finished being the negotiator."

"As you wish," he quietly replied.

He appeared next to Gabriel and relayed all that he had told me to them, then I informed him of what had happened with Lillith and Adam. I was utterly surprised at how calm Lucifer remained through the whole thing. Once we finished he stood completely still, his golden eyes slowly becoming brittle and cold. Fear started to take hold of me. Lucifer was not calm, his anger had far exceeded the desire or ability to irrationally lash out at the world around him.

"So I am evil am I?" It was a question but he enunciated it as a threat.

"What exactly is evil?" Gabriel asked.

Uriel shrugged, "Apparently whatever Elohim says it is."

Elohim's actions had overshadowed Lucifer's description of the bond between he and Lillith but Gabriel was not about to let it go undiscussed. "This bond with you and Lillith. Remiel suggested destroying anything unbalanced that Elohim has created. If we destroy Lillith how will that affect you?"

Gabriel was usually much more tactful than that, "Gabriel!" I started to try to explain things but Lucifer's aura exploded, wind raged around us, trees were ripped from the roots and clouds gathered above us.

"Your solution to Elohim's actions are to threaten Lillith?" His voice was eerily quiet and in complete contrast to the storm that swelled and raged around us.

"I also stated that Adam and Lillith are no threat to us," I replied in the same tone of voice he was using, "Gabriel failed to mention that. I do not think their destruction will serve any greater purpose, not when Elohim is creating something that seems to be designed to confront us directly."

"He did say that," Uriel confirmed.

Lucifer stepped closer to me, "Remiel, do you remember I told you that you would all be forced to choose sides? When I told you I would not be made to subjugate myself to him? You dismissed my concerns. This is that moment. Do you understand now? Do you see the full extent of his madness? He will not stop, will not be dissuaded or bargained with. He no longer cares for the balance brothers. There is only his need to rule, those that support him will be welcomed, those that do not support him he will try to destroy."

The whole time he had been speaking the storm had grown in intensity. As he spoke his last words hail mixed with fire hurtled towards the ground.

He raised his face to the sky, his aura sparking and destroying each and every hail stone or bit of fire that touched it, "If Elohim wishes to call me evil, so be it. He is the one who has destroyed all that was good, not I. I have kept my word and not raised a hand against him, no longer. Everything in creation has an opposite, it is time that he is reminded of that."

Flickering golden eyes focused back on us, "Lillith is not to be harmed, I will protect her even if none of you will. Choose where you shall stand in this brothers. The time for talking is over."

CHAPTER 13

He left before I could reply and the hailstorm ended as quickly as it had come.

"He is going after Elohim!" Uriel shouted and flickered out as well. I heard him reach out the rest of us. "Brothers! Hurry!"

Gabriel and I exchanged a horrified look and followed Uriel. We were almost blinded when we reached our destination. Elohim and Lucifer's battle had begun and the entirety of creation was at stake. They were as bright as the stars that surrounded them, Lucifer shone more intensely then every sunset that had ever existed since we first started our task and Elohim set the darkness of space on fire. Bolts of lightning and flame arced between them. As they dodged I could feel them weaving defenses around themselves, pulling upon the lines of power, distorting them in ways that they had never been intended for.

Lucifer reached his hand out, clenched it tight and Elohim screamed, his voice shattering our ears. I shifted my perceptions and saw that Lucifer had somehow bound Elohim as I had tried to do to him when we fought. A net of writhing, twisting power gripped Elohim who struggled against it. Lucifer's face twisted with the effort as he pulled his arm to the side then explosively released his power, hurtling Elohim into a small moon that was nearby.

"No!" Seraqual cried in absolute shock and horror as he manifested at the exact moment that Elohim went crashing into the moon and Lucifer barreled after him. The rest of my brothers, except Michael, appeared as the two of them crashed into the surface of the moon and we felt a monstrous surge of power which threw all of us back.

Raguel crashed into me, righted himself and spun. "Now what?" He demanded, "What set this off?"

"All of you listen." I replied and sent the entirety of all of our recent exchanges directly into their minds, "Discuss later. We have to stop this. Raphael, Raguel, Seraqual, Gabriel, see to that moon." Whatever had caused that surge of power had pushed the moon out of it's proper position.

"The rest of us have to.." Another wave of power rocketed through us, "What are they doing?!" It felt like Elohim was trying to pull another planet towards the moon they were on. Uriel and I acted as one and threw ourselves towards Elohim and Lucifer.

"Stop!" Uriel ordered but they were too far gone in their hate. They were standing in the immense and newly formed crater that their impact had created. Flames, lightning, hail, driving rain, rocks and unseen energy surged between the two. The ground around Elohim had turned molten, surging around his feet and driving towards Lucifer who was encased in a shield of swirling colors. Elohim's madness had completely overtaken him, distorting his features into something wholly unrecognizable.

"This is futile Lucifer!" he spat out. "You cannot destroy me. I am the giver of life. What happens to your precious balance without that?"

"The balance has already been destroyed," Lucifer hissed out. "You have done that, not I. Life will go on with or without you Elohim. Even if it doesn't, it is better if it dies out free from your madness."

Elohim's eyes burned. He raised his hands and the molten earth below him shot up and towards Lucifer. Lucifer's eyes narrowed and he vanished, leaving Elohim's lava to shoot far past where he had been standing and tear another hole into the moon. Lucifer reappeared behind Elohim and drove his hand into Elohim's side just as a bronze and gold streak came shooting through the air towards them.

Uriel made as if to intercept Michael but I stopped him, "Michael! Don't!" He cried.

Elohim screeched as Lucifer's hand sunk farther into him. He twisted in Lucifer's grip and was about to attack when Michael's streaking form shifted into a lance that drove through both of them and out the other side.

Existence shuddered, all of us screamed in pain, Elohim and Lucifer collapsed. Michael manifested, fully cloaked in golden armor, reached his arms out and wrapped his hands around their throats. He slowly pulled them to their feet, gripping ever and ever tighter. Elohim made as if to strike Michael but was instantly restrained by coiled, bronze burning ropes of power, Elohim went limp. Lucifer just waited.

"I care little for your new creations on that planet," Michael said, his anger sending vibrations through all of us, "I care even less for your dispute and I am coming to care less and less for either of you. What I do care about is ensuring that your insanity does not destroy the entirety of creation." He lifted the both of them higher off the ground, "We shall resolve this now and if either of you do this again in the future I will not hesitate to do what is needed." His head turned towards me, "Remiel, I did not quite understand everything you tried to relay to me. I was busy elsewhere and missed some of it. Please explain."

I did as he asked and left nothing out. Several moments of silence passed after I finished and I could feel Elohim and Lucifer recovering their strength. They would soon be able to break free from Michael and start up again.

"Lucifer," Michael spoke, "You state you will protect Lillith at all costs. Why? Why not Adam as well?"

"I care for her." Lucifer stated simply. "She has become as precious to me as you are. I know it is not right but it is the truth. Release me, I will not strike you Michael."

The armor that had encased Michael's face faded. Eyes as hard as the emeralds appeared and there was little doubt that he was well aware that his ability to hold the two of them was quickly fading. He released his hold on Lucifer and turned all his attention to Elohim, the bronze coils flared in power but Elohim merely smiled.

"Explain yourself." Michael ordered, "You violated the spirit of the promise you made to us. You contacted Adam and deceived me in doing so. What is this creation that Remiel destroyed?"

There was a hint in his tone that this offense hurt him much more than the previous ones.

"Lucifer has his bond to Lillith," Elohim replied, "I chose not to give Adam a spark of myself, unlike our impetuous brother but it was hardly fair to leave Adam without any assistance at all. I was merely making sure he knew his role. What Remiel destroyed? I knew, yet again, none of you would care as to my reasons for what I did and would attack me. Since all of you have seen fit to view me as an enemy I decided I should make something that I could trust to defend me."

Michael flinched and released Elohim. "I only attacked you because you and Lucifer were threatening everything." Michael pointed out.

Elohim nodded, a veneer of understanding attempted to hide his arrogance. "Of course Michael. I know you were forced into this."

Lucifer growled, "Will you keep allowing him to fool you Michael? Can you not see what he has done?"

"What I see Lucifer is that he has merely done what you already did. Deceived all of us about your true intentions with these creations." He shook his head, "I only wish I could destroy both of them and your knowledge of how to make them." His voice went from resigned to resolved. As he spoke his right arm became encased in a vibrant golden shaft of light, the armor encased his face once again and his aura completely solidified around him. "As that is not possible and neither of you can be trusted any further I will simply state this. Hate each other, scheme all you like, twist Adam and Lillith into whatever perversions suit you, but know this," Every line of energy around us swirled and shifted as, slowly spiraling around him. He slammed the shaft of light that encased his arm into the ground, instantly solidifying the lava that Elohim had created during the fight. Shock waves of the force of his blow reverberated through the core of the planet throwing it back into it's proper alignment. "If either of you, ever again, let things get this far I will do what I must to stop you. I care not what that will be." His words and the force of his power echoed through us even after he left.

Lucifer and Elohim stared at each other. "I wonder," Elohim mused, "Did she feel everything you just did dearest Lucifer? Do you think she survived?"

Lucifer froze, "No," he whispered, he started to shift.

"How much of what she feels do you feel brother?" There was no disguising his intent and I found myself standing next to a frozen Lucifer, utter desolation and darkness radiating from him.

"There is no point in asking what you mean Elohim," I said, "Your actions speak for themselves. An attack upon Lillith to get to Lucifer is an attack upon me as well. Am I clear?"

"And the rest of you?" Elohim gestured grandly towards the rest of my brothers. "Where do you stand in this? With Michael, Lucifer or myself?"

Uriel joined me, so did Raguel. Gabriel and Seraqual looked helplessly between us and Raphael spoke. "I am with Michael. Only call upon me Uriel when there is a task that needs doing. I care little for the company of any of you at this point." He shimmered and faded from our sight.

Elohim looked at Gabriel and Seraqual, "You are too cowardly to choose I see. I'll make it simple for you then. Since you have not chosen to stand at my side I shall assume that you will work against me." He sighed and shook his head, "Really, this would have been so much easier if you would have accepted the truth. Uriel, I hope that the universe no longer requires my assistance because I shall be busy elsewhere. I have my own world to shape." He smiled and left.

"I can barely feel her," Lucifer said, then he shifted, leaving the rest of us standing on the destroyed surface of a moon.

I ached, Michael's attack upon them had ripped through all of us in some way and now that the imminent threat was over the pain crashed into me. Uriel sagged next to me causing Raguel to brace him. Gabriel and Seraqual slowly crumpled to the ground. Words failed all of us for quite some time.

Eventually Gabriel spoke, "What do we do now?"

"Nothing," I answered, "There is nothing that can be done. We have tried everything. Lucifer and Elohim will never reconcile. Brothers, we have to prepare ourselves, this will happen again."

"Michael will stand by his word," Uriel said. "He has the power to harm them. He is close to their equal and he has always had something about him that makes him stronger in some way."

"Yes. I know," I replied.

"Tell me again about this creation you destroyed Remiel?" Raguel asked.

As I spoke he grew increasingly thoughtful and concerned. "It did exactly what he said, when he said?" He asked.

"Yes. Why?"

He slammed his fist into the ground, "He will make more of them and send them against us," he paused and I felt him searching for Elohim, a puzzled look crossed his face then he started to panic. "I cannot find him. Uriel?"

We all reached out and found every one of our brothers but Elohim. "How?" Raquel demanded.

"Lucifer had figured something similar out. I told you how he was hiding his bond from us," I answered. "Apparently Elohim has taken it much further."

"We have to get to Lillith then," Uriel stated and stood up.

132

"Why?" Gabriel asked. "Lucifer is with her. I see no reason for us to go."

"That is why we need to go." Uriel explained. "Elohim's comment about his own world to create? What do you think he was referring to? He will go after that world and Lucifer will try to stop him. We have to do what we can to keep them from coming to blows again, somehow."

Gabriel looked at each of us in turn and I watched as he put walls around his heart. "No Uriel. I want nothing more to do with this. I will not be party to harming either of my brothers."

"Gabriel!" Raguel snapped, "So you're willing to let them tear everything apart? Is that it?"

"I..I..." He started trembling.

"Peace Raguel," I said. I drew closer to Gabriel and placed my hand on his shoulder. "Gabriel, I understand. We all must choose what feels right to us."

His eyes were downcast as he spoke, "Thank you. I am sorry."

After he left Seraqual spoke. His eyes were closed and each word he said was delivered very precisely as if he was controlling a great need to destroy something, "They tried to destroy two planets. Look at what they did here. If Michael had not intervened, how much worse would it have been?"

"Brother?" Uriel asked gently.

"I am with Michael but I will come with you. This must not be allowed to happen, ever, again. If Elohim wants one world, he will soon want another and another." As his eyes opened his aura flared around him. "Lucifer was right, choices must be made."

The four of us found Lucifer and sent ourselves to him.

"Lillith!" I was stunned when I saw them. He was cradling her in his arms, tears were streaming down her face and she was in tremendous pain although there were no obvious wounds on her.

133

"Why does it hurt?" She managed to get out in between pained gasps, "Lucifer, help."

"I am sorry, so sorry." He pressed his face to her head and clutched her tighter, "You are not wounded, it will pass. I promise."

I looked closer at him. He was still recovering, somehow he and Elohim had given the appearance of being much stronger than they truly were after Michael's attack. If Michael had attacked me in such a way I would have been dead again, and I had had to help Uriel heal after Elohim wounded him. I was beginning to realize just how much stronger Elohim, Lucifer and Michael were than I. I had always known, on some level, that they were more powerful than I but the differences were becoming much more clear.

"I can help," I offered.

"No," Lucifer whispered, "It will just tie you to her Remiel. One of us is enough, please. Let me rest. The faster I heal, the sooner she will stop suffering."

"Elohim will be coming here," Raguel stated.

Lucifer looked up at us and I stepped back. The only thing keeping him from calling another hail storm at that moment was that Lillith was in his arms.

"Later Raguel," I said, "Let him rest, Elohim is probably still recovering as well. Come." I led them away and we waited in silence, consumed with our own thoughts as to what the future might bring.

CHAPTER 14

Several minutes passed, Raguel looked at me, "Where's Adam? One would think he would have been here comforting Lillith."

"He may have been but when Lucifer appeared he probably ran," I replied. "Remember he thinks Lucifer is evil."

"But he has never seen Lucifer before," Uriel pointed out.

"Lillith would have cried out to him when her pain started and when he appeared," I said, "If the amount of pain she is in now after Lucifer has healed some is any indication, what she felt prior to that would have been much more severe." I looked over my shoulder at the two of them. Her eyes were closed, the tension had eased slightly from her body. He was running his hands through her hair while rocking her back and forth as gently as he could. It appeared that he had made her fall asleep to ease her pain. I sent out a thought and found Adam in the woods not too far away. "A moment brothers, I found Adam. I'll see what state he is in."

Uriel placed a hand on my arm, "Wait Remiel. We need to decide if getting further involved with these creations is the wisest course."

"If Elohim is intent on somehow controlling Adam shouldn't we try to prevent that?" I asked.

"No," Raguel stated. "Look where that has gotten us so far." He said with a gesture towards Lillith and Lucifer. "Our family is shattered, the balance is lost. The more we care about Adam and Lillith the worse it will get. We will become more splintered and take further sides in this. Michael had a point. Let Lucifer and Elohim do what they wish with them, we have to confine their battles to this one world. We are in charge of the whole of the universe, not just this planet."

I had to admit that Raguel was right. We had no idea where Elohim was or what he was doing. if we interfered with Adam it would only compound the insult Lucifer had already delivered. Adam was not our concern. Technically neither was Lillith but since she was so intertwined with Lucifer we couldn't abandon her, or at least, I couldn't.

"Very well. I concede your point Raguel," I said. "How do you propose to keep the battle to here?"

"I.." Raguel began to speak when Lucifer's voice came from behind us.

"I will not confront him directly in the future," he said, causing all of us to turn around. "If I were to do so again, nothing, not even Michael would be able to stop us and Raguel is correct. There are greater concerns for you than this world." There was an emptiness within him that had never been there before, his anger had settled into something much darker, much more dangerous then what had driven him against Elohim earlier. At that moment I knew that we had truly lost him as a brother. Who Lucifer had been in the past had been twisted, changed, lost. "He will return here, to Adam, to what he considers is his world to rule. Adam may not have Elohim's energy as Lillith does mine but his need for Adam is no less. I will keep him confined to this world."

"How brother?" Uriel asked.

Gently, with great care, he placed Lillith on the ground and stood up. As he did the sky darkened once again, he flared his aura out over Lillith, protecting her from the approaching storm. His aura's usual sunset purples were so dark as to appear almost black, "Simple Uriel. By corrupting everything he makes to worship him, turning every creature against him, stripping him of their forced love for him and freeing them. He will be so consumed with hate for me that he will turn a blind eye to the rest of the universe."

"What's to keep him from confronting you directly?" Seraqual asked in hushed tones.

He bared his teeth in disgust, "His own cowardice. Since this began he has always fled when confronted. When I went after him he tried to hide from me, but I followed. He was cornered and had no choice but to fight back. Michael's intervention saved him and he is well aware of it. He will never attack me. He knows if he does that will bring Michael's wrath down upon him as well as my own."

"Why must you do this?" Uriel asked. "Take her elsewhere, leave him to this obsession of his. You need not become even more hated by him. What is the point?"

"All of you," he replied, the slightest hint of love for us still in his voice, "You are the point, you along with Lillith. Has he not declared that those of you who don't stand with him against him? Raphael informed me of what Elohim had stated after I left. I cannot leave her unguarded. She is a weakness in me that he will exploit, just as all of you can be used against each other if he is given a chance. No, it is best for him to have one enemy," That darkness that I had begun to feel in him came pouring out, the sense of his entire being shifted, "And I am the one best suited for it, he has already deemed me evil after all. In keeping him focused on me, on my supposed betrayals of him he will think of nothing else. His anger towards you will fade, you can continue to do such tasks as you are able. Believe me brothers, this is the best way."

"You're trying to cloak your own hate of him within this offer of yours," Raguel challenged, "You want to destroy him. There is no honor in this, no sacrifice on your part."

"When did I say there was?" Lucifer replied in that frightfully calm voice. "Where did I give the impression to you that this was about honor or sacrifice? I am offering a solution to this problem. My motivations in doing so are truly none of your concern. All of that aside Raguel, what other options do you have? None of you are threats to him and it seems that he has simply dismissed you at this point. If he is making more of those things that Remiel destroyed and sends them after you, what then? A never ending battle that scars existence from one end to the other? No!" Even though he had not moved from Lillith's side it felt as if he were directly in front of me, inches from my face. The potency of his words, even spoken softly, was that strong. "I will not lie Raguel, I have come to hate him but I would rather spend eternity here, on this planet, using my hate to keep him from befouling everything then take Lillith elsewhere and trying to hide her from him. Such actions will just cause greater harm and schisms between all of us."

"So you would leave us, leave everything to stay here? With her and your hate?" Serqual asked.

He didn't respond. Seraqual crossed the distance between Lucifer and us, and knelt down next to Lillith. "Is this how you choose to show your love for her? Does any creation deserve what you two are planning? I agree with Michael that whatever it is you choose to do to these creations is between you and Elohim. But this? This Lucifer? You are no better than he is if you are dedicating yourself to corrupting them for your own revenge. He wants to rule and you wish nothing but to subvert and destroy. I will not be a party to this, to any of it. You should destroy her now, it will show more love of her than further embroiling her in this conflict." He brushed her arm with his hand, bowed his head for a moment and stood up. "Is this your choice then?"

Lucifer merely nodded. Seraqual closed his eyes in sorrow. "I shall miss you, miss calling you brother, miss the exquisite creations you have made. To turn such a gift towards something like this...." he opened his eyes, shook his head and left.

Lucifer's face stayed empty, as if Seraqual's words had no effect upon him but we all knew differently. None of us wanted to speak because we all knew that Seraqual spoke the truth. Lucifer's declaration, once again, shifted our opinions. There was no right or wrong side anymore. This had turned into a personal vendetta between them and the grand ideals of free will versus no will had been tarnished. Uriel and Raguel looked at me and I kept my eyes fixed upon Lucifer. I forced myself to start thinking past Lucifer and Elohim as my brothers and try to see where things were heading. I had no doubt that Elohim was making more of what I had destroyed and with Lucifer's decision I knew more violence would erupt in the near future. I had no idea who would start it but I wanted to be prepared this time.

"I will not defend you Lucifer, not any longer," I stated, that made his control over his emotions slip and I saw what impact my words had. " I will also not condemn you. We are beyond that now. I agree with you that Elohim will return and I agree that your mutual hatred for each other will keep him occupied. It is better if that is limited to here than spread all over the universe. I also wish to be more prepared this time. This is my choice then, I will keep track of Adam as I am sure Elohim will keep speaking to him. Lucifer, you said you could follow Elohim when he tried to get away from you. Had he disappeared as he has now?"

"Disappeared? What do you mean?"

"Try to find him," I directed. It was immediately evident that Lucifer, like us, had failed to locate him.

"No, he hadn't concealed himself as well as he is now."

"Can you give us an idea on how to find him?" Uriel asked, "You were masking your bond with Lillith. Is he doing something similar?"

"Perhaps," Lucifer replied, his face became more animated as he addressed this new challenge, "But without knowing where he is I cannot be sure of how he is concealing himself. I mirrored the world around me, he could be doing something completely different."

"Uriel, Raguel. We have to find Elohim and try to see what he is doing."

"Why?" Raguel asked, "Those things he made are no match for us. If he sends them here, he and Lucifer can battle it out here. It's not our issue."

"We are all assuming that Elohim is not crafting things like Lillith on other worlds." Uriel pointed out, "Or perhaps things even more powerful. That thing Remiel destroyed was his first attempt. What if he had truly given it his spark?"

Raguel clenched his fists, "Fine. I see your point." He shifted his eyes and looked at Lucifer, "You, I want to despise you brother. I truly do but I can't." He sighed and relaxed his hands, "None of us knew that this would be the result of what you did. I can't blame you for your hate towards Elohim because he has made it clear that he cares little for us. You tried, in your own way, to keep your word. I won't condemn you for what led you and us here. I also can't agree with what you propose to do to keep Elohim busy, but...." he paused, made his way to Lucifer and embraced him, "but if it works, it's a better alternative than anything else. I won't forgive you but there is little to be gained by holding it against you either."

He stepped back, Lucifer nodded and looked at Uriel.

"Will you help us if we call for you?" Uriel asked. "Or will you merely sit here and wait for Elohim?"

Lucifer looked at Lillith, then back to us. "I will find a way to keep her safe and aid you if you require. Especially if Elohim attacks any of you. I will also do what tasks I can."

"Fine. Then I still consider you a brother. I, like the others, cannot condone what you are proposing for the future but if that remains here and only here, then I shan't move against you."

"I understand," Lucifer replied.

"Good," Uriel stated than moved on to planning. "Remiel, stay with Adam. Lucifer, explain to Raguel and I how you were hiding your bond and other ways you think Elohim could be doing this. Then he and I will relay the information to the others. They can join in the hunt or not but they should at least know what to look for. Agreed?"

We all nodded. I located Adam again, turned myself invisible to his eyes and left them. Once I reached where Adam was I put my hand to his head and sent him to sleep as Lucifer had done to Lillith numerous times. It was remarkably easy. As soon as that was done all the things I had wanted to say to Lucifer came out of my mouth.

"How dare you! You propose to further profane a creation in an attempt to keep the battle limited to here! Can you not see all the dangers inherent in that? And Elohim! Deeming us enemies for not bowing down to your wishes! Where have my brothers gone? This makes no sense!" I went on and on for quite some time. I hadn't spoken them to Lucifer because I knew that my words would fall on deaf ears. Elohim had pushed him too far. Once Lucifer was driven to attack it was too late, he would never back down now.

As I wound down Adam started stirring and mumbling in his sleep. "Yes Great One, I understand. She is no longer worthy of me."

What was this?

"A new mate. One that is not tainted. Thank you." He rolled over and lapsed back into silence.

Now what was Elohim planning?

CHAPTER 15

Adam stayed silent the rest of the time he slept. When he awakened he headed away from where Lillith and Lucifer had been and found some food. He didn't seem the least bit concerned for Lillith and went about his day with no further communication from Elohim. I found this troublesome as it appeared that he had formed no bond with her. I wasn't sure how much of that was due to her the bond she already had with Lucifer or how much was Elohim's doing. Back then, the mysteries of human emotions and how humans choose mates were even further beyond us. Even after all this time I still am not sure how that works.

I spent the day with Adam but gained no further insight into Elohim's plans or location. As the sun began to set I had calmed down enough to be able to speak with Lucifer again and sent a thought in his direction. "How is she?"

"She has recovered," he replied. "As have I. Thank you for asking."

"Adam said something earlier, in his sleep. Elohim appears to be making him a new mate."

I hadn't been sure what to expect when Lucifer heard the news. His lack of response made it clear that he was just as confused about it as I was.

"Did he say why?" he asked.

"It appears Elohim views her as tainted." I was surprised how calm he remained. Perhaps he had reached the point where he was no longer surprised what Elohim would accuse him of.

"Truly? A new mate?"

A sense of eagerness resounded within him but it wasn't filled with joy and excitement. I have watched many predators hunt and that pivotal moment right before they commit in full to the lunge or strike, that is how Lucifer felt.

"Will you inform her?" I asked. Silence greeted my question.

"I must take some time to decide what is best. Thank you for the information," he replied then brushed the topic aside, "I informed Uriel how I hid the bond between she and I. He relayed it to the others then left. Perhaps you should speak with him and see if he needs assistance. I have other things to attend to."

His tone left little question that he was drawing the line as to what he would partake in. Since he felt that the conversation needed to end and I had little desire in pursuing anything further I reached out, found Uriel and left without another word.

Uriel, myself, Raguel, Michael and a rather grudging Gabriel spent a great deal of time searching for Elohim. Raphael and Seraqual chose to remain apart from the rest of us and we respected their decision. Michael assisted more out of concern that Elohim was creating a great numbers of the creatures I destroyed than any real desire to find Elohim. We all reacted differently to what had transpired. The split between Elohim and Lucifer felt in many ways like we had suffered two deaths in the family. Myself, Uriel and Michael forced ourselves to stay occupied. When we weren't looking for Elohim we did what tasks we could. Raguel built a wall of stone around what he was feeling, his remarks became sharper and more hurtful and Gabriel hovered on the edge of silence for quite some time. He only spoke when spoken to and took much longer to complete things than was normal for him. All of us avoided Lucifer while we searched for Elohim.

Whatever Elohim was doing allowed him to elude us for quite some time. When he finally reappeared to us we gathered together before rushing to where we sensed him to be.

"He is on the same planet as they are," Uriel said. "There is something else too."

Michael shook his head, clenched his fist and his arm became enveloped in golden light. "He made more."

143

"Yes," I felt it as well. "They are stronger than the one I destroyed."

Raphael and Seraqual appeared next to Michael. "We are here to make sure whatever conflict occurs stays on that world," Raphael stated, "We will not take sides."

We looked at each other, "If he does not attack us should we get involved?" Gabriel asked. "The two of them are the ones in conflict, not us."

"Yes." Michael replied. "Elohim has created things that are immensely strong now. He needs to be shown that we will not allow him to spread them throughout the universe."

"Let us see what he has to say first Michael," Uriel stated. "He does not seem to be threatening Lucifer with them yet. They are on opposite sides of the world at the moment. If we go in there and just attack these creations it is not likely to solve anything and will most likely make things worse."

Michael said nothing in reply.

"Lucifer showed us how to hide ourselves well enough," Seraqual stated, "Instead of speaking to him we could go down there and watch whatever it is he is doing. I am not sure I could stand another conversation with either of them."

"So we lower ourselves to their level?" Michael snarled, "Hiding and lying?"

"I do not like it anymore than you do," I countered. "But it is perhaps the only way we will find out the truth. He seems to feel that we do nothing but betray and mock him so why would he enlighten us to what he is planning."

Michael tightened his jaw, bronze colored armor surrounded him again and scowled at us, "Brothers, are the rest of you in agreement?"

Hesitant nods came from the remains of my family, "Fine," He growled, "Let us cower in the shadows then."

We shifted into pure energy and with silent thoughts decided who would go where to spy on Elohim and his new creations, mirrored the world around us, blended and listened. I hovered by a winged human like creation that bore more than a passing resemblance to Michael's appearance in his walking around form, same red hair, same green eyes. It's wings were white and stretched from it's heels to well above it's head. It stood at the edge of a large forest, some sort of weapon in hand and appeared to be guarding the forest from intruders. It's face was blank although it's dark green eyes never stopped moving from side to side. I drew closer to it, it tensed and turned it's head in my direction. I moved several feet in either direction. It looked confused as if it felt that I was there but since it could not actually see me was unsure as what actions it should take. I flowed into the nearest tree, becoming one with it in such a way that only my brothers should be able to sense me. The winged creature's eyes slowly shifted as it narrowed it's eyes in thought.

"Father, I sense something." It spoke. It's eyes widened and it nodded it's head as if someone was speaking to it. "It's gone now but I felt I needed to inform you. Thank you. I live to serve." It relaxed and resumed looking off into the distance.

"Remiel," Michael's astonished voice whispered to me, "They can sense us."

"I know. Meld into a tree or rock. That seems to block their ability to feel our presence."

"This one looks like you," Michael continued.

"I am looking at a rougher version of you with wings at the moment."

"What is this?" Seraqual's horrified voice reached me. "There are seven of them aren't there?"

"Yes," Uriel confirmed. "Come to me. Elohim has appeared, with Adam and a female who is not Lillith."

"He will sense us," I pointed out.

"Remiel, he already knows we are here. We were not skilled enough at hiding it seems. Come."

We joined Uriel. As soon as we manifested the two creations that stood on either side of Elohim stepped forward, placing themselves between Elohim and us. One had Lucifer's pale gold hair and the other reminded me of Uriel.

Michael's aura flared, a spear appeared in his hand. "You dare?"

Elohim ignored us and turned Adam and the new female towards the forest. "This is your world my children, your garden of safety. Because I love and cherish you I am gifting you with this. Here you will be safe from harm, from tainting. I have created guardians for you. They shall watch over you when I cannot. If you are ever in danger just call for them and they will appear to help you. All I ask in return my children is that you always love me and listen to me, that you do what I say for I created you and know what's best for you."

"Of course Great One," Adam replied.

"Now what of these others?" Elohim gestured to us.

The female spoke, "They are not to be trusted. They betrayed you and will lead us astray. You created us and love us."

Elohim finally looked at us, his lips twisted into a smile laden with superiority and utter dismissal of us. "Indeed, Eve. Well done. Go now. Explore the world I have gifted you. Everything you shall need is there."

Adam and Eve bowed to him and walked away. None of us could manage to speak a single word. Elohim watched us for a few moments then walked in between his winged creations and up to Michael.

"The strongest one I made in your image. When you pierced both Lucifer and I earlier, I knew you would never join me. You, however, were the only one who hadn't outright condemned me or thought me mad. I wanted to honor that."

Michael stepped away from him, "You are mad. I did not want to see it before, but now I have no choice." He leveled his spear towards Elohim's chest. The rest of us moved away. Lavender tinted my vision, power vibrated from my hands. The air crackled and hissed as all my brothers flared their auras and prepared for a battle.

Elohim threw his head back, laughed and raised his hand. The sound of wings hammered the air around us and we were surrounded by his creations, their weapons were drawn and power resonated between them and him. "Individually they are weaker than you, but together and with me here it is a much different situation," Elohim stated.

"Interesting," Lucifer's calm, cold voice came from behind Elohim. "They failed to sense me though. Your skills are still lacking."

Instantly Elohim spun and all seven of his creations shifted to surround Lucifer instead of us. Lucifer eyed the one that most resembled him, "I am disappointed brother," Condescension dripped from his words, "I would have thought you would have made this one more hideous and used it as some sort of thing to scare them."

"You may have betrayed me Lucifer," Elohim replied, his tone wary. "But without you I could not have created either Adam, Eve or these masterpieces."

"Ah," Lucifer said as he walked closer towards it, "So you wanted to honor me as you did Michael?"

"Perhaps." Elohim made a small gesture and it lunged towards Lucifer lifted his hand and Elohim's creation was stopped mid stride and slowly rose above the ground.

"Father!" It cried as it struggled against Lucifer's hold.

"Well?" Lucifer taunted. "Do you truly care for this thing Elohim or will you merely discard it and build another one if I destroy it?"

We felt Lucifer's power build and it started to shriek as it's wings turned black and it's feet started to resemble hooves.

"No!" Elohim raged and the rest of his winged guardians surged towards Lucifer, but to no avail. Lucifer merely shifted out of their way while continuing to corrupt the one he was holding. Surging walls of blazing energy erupted from Elohim. We all sensed where Lucifer was going to appear next, or so we thought. Elohim spun and violently flung his arm out. A tree trunk thick stream of molten energy flowed towards where he sensed Lucifer would be but Lucifer did not appear, the creation did.

It's skin was the color of charred wood, the night black wings engulfed the ground around it in shadows and it's hands had been turned into misshapen claws. Yet it's face was the most horrendous change of all. Lucifer had made it beautiful, a mirror image of his own, but had somehow stripped it of all rational thought and filled it with violence and hate. It bounded out of the way of Elohim's power and drove itself with immense wing strokes directly at him. Elohim's version of Michael intercepted it, it's sword taking the corrupted one in the chest. The scream it emitted was not filled with pain, but with a lust for battle. It grabbed the sword from the other one's hand and ripped the sword from it's chest then plunged it into the chest of the one that resembled Michael, locking eyes with Elohim as it did so.

"Enough!" Elohim snapped, "I made you! You belong to me!"

We felt Elohim reach out and try to force his will onto it. The corrupted one paused, dropped the sword and flung it's hands over it's ears. "What's happening to me? Father help!" It dropped to it's knees, shuddering, then slowly collapsed in pain.

Lucifer's dark laugh caressed the air around us although we could not see him. "As I said Elohim, your skills are still lacking. He's a much better representation of me now. None of your creations are safe from me, brother. They never will be."

Elohim clenched his fists, "My skills are lacking?" he spat out. "You only corrupt the greatness that I create. You are nothing without me! All of you are nothing!" He stalked to the one that looked like Michael, it had crumpled onto it's side as blood flowed from it's chest. Elohim bent down, healed it's wound and handed it the sword, "Kill the tainted one," he commanded. It pushed it's way to it's feet, flexed it wings and plunged the sword through the chest of the corrupted one who gasped as all it's muscles tightened for a brief moment, then went limp.

"The universe means nothing to me now." Elohim declared, "I have my own world, my own universe to control. If Lucifer or any of you try to take that from me, I will destroy everything we have ever created."

Lucifer manifested in front of us, facing Elohim. "You lack the courage to do that Elohim. You refuse to attack me, much less Michael or the rest. Fear not, they will not harm you or your world. That is my task, one that I shall dedicate the rest of eternity to. Unless you'd like to finish this once and for all." As he spoke those words the air around him erupted into lighting and hail. Elohim's creations covered themselves with their wings to protect their skin from assault of ice and exploding earth as lighting struck the ground around us.

Elohim's eyes dropped from Lucifer and landed on the body of his creation that Lucifer had corrupted in mere minutes. He looked at us, then at his remaining guardians. The numbers were not in his favor and he knew it. His creation of his guardians had solidified us against him. I was never sure why he thought that there could have be any other outcome once he had taken that step. He turned away from us, his guardians did the same. Lucifer brought the hail and lighting to an end.

"As I thought. Practice your skills Elohim, perhaps one day you will create something that I will not be able to turn against you." He looked over his shoulder, his eyes were empty as he met our eyes. "Leave brothers. You have other things to attend to."

What choice did we have?

CHAPTER 16

We did not truly leave, we merely relocated to another area of the world and stared, dumbfounded at each other.

Raphael sunk to the ground, eyes wide with astonishment, "How did he?"

"Why would he?" Gabriel hissed.

Uriel started to pace, "What Eve said troubles me."

"Troubles?" Michael hissed. "That is not the word I would use to describe what just happened."

"Are they truly so much more powerful than we?" Seraqual murmured.

"They are applying their strengths to things we never contemplated." Raquel muttered as he joined Uriel in pacing.

I just stood there, silent. There were no words for me. I had tried to prevent this. That moment when I first felt an abyss opening below me, when Gabriel and I had spoken after Lillith first awakened. It seemed so distant while simultaneously feeling like it happened mere hours ago. Every moment, every word, every incident between then and now, I sifted through them, searching for an answer, a reason. Nothing came to me. No reason, no answer, no logic could be twisted and bent to fit what I had just witnessed.

"It is over brothers," I said. I could not look at them as I spoke. I fixed my eyes on the horizon, searching for a reason out among the distant planets.

Uriel stopped pacing and lowered his head, "Is there nothing left Remiel? Nothing we can do?"

"We cannot kill Lucifer or Elohim and destroying Lillith, Adam or Eve will only enrage them further." I stated. "We leave this planet to them, to their hate of each other. We must move on and

150

do what we can elsewhere while protecting the rest of creation from them. Lucifer's statement that Elohim's hate of him will keep Elohim from spreading his madness seems accurate, for now. A few eons from now, we cannot know." I shrugged and looked at Michael. "Your option is all that is left Michael."

"Both of them disgust me at this point," Michael replied. "The less I have to do with either of them the better. What about those winged abominations that Elohim created?"

"Leave them to me." Lucifer's voice echoed in our minds. I saw him first. He had chosen to appear a fair distance away from us but well within my line of sight. "Farewell brothers," he continued. "If you are ever forced to come in conflict with me in the future, I will bear you no ill will. My choices brought me here. If there are to be further consequences I accept them." He did not flare his aura or make any grand displays. He merely looked at each of us in turn, nodded once and left.

We took one last look at this world that had held such great joy for us and one by one we left without any further words.

If you have read this in full I realize it must shock you, confuse you and perhaps even enrage you. It is the truth, which is rarely of true comfort. I will share one more truth with you and it will be even less comforting than what has preceded it. It was not Lucifer that tainted Eve. It was Lillith and it happened completely by accident.

It took years before I was able to bring myself to contemplate speaking to Lucifer again. Perhaps you wonder how I could after everything that had transpired. He was my brother and had been since the first sun flared into existence, I could no more disavow him then I could sever a limb from myself. Several of the others were less forgiving than I, but I never pushed them either way. Aside from missing my brother, I found I felt a nagging curiosity to see what Lillith had accomplished. I missed her joy of life and excitement. My tasks held little joy or sense of accomplishment

151

for me anymore. There were so many things I could not complete since we could not truly bring animals into existence, not without Elohim. That was why I found myself reaching out to find her or Lucifer one day and sending myself to them.

For whatever reason Lucifer was not concealing their presence. I chose to send a thought out to Lucifer before fully manifesting in front of them. He may not want to see me and I had no idea what had transpired between he and Elohim after we had left.

"Lucifer?" There was a considerable pause before he replied.

"Remiel? Why are you speaking to me? Has something happened?" He was not angry with me but he was wary.

I felt uncomfortable speaking to him. As if I was intruding somewhere I was not wanted. "No. I..."

"Yes?"

"I...wish to see you and Lillith." Once I got the words out it seemed utterly foolish to have said them. What came back to me wasn't words, it was a sense of relief, of sadness and an invitation. "If that will be acceptable to both of you of course."

"Yes. Lillith would love to see you...and..." he paused.

My foolishness left me and was replaced by a hint of joy. "Thank you." I sent myself to them and before I even finished solidifying my form Lillith had thrown her arms around me.

"Remiel!" That joy of life that I had remembered was still there. I returned her embrace and stepped back to look at them, and was rendered instantly speechless when I did so. Lillith's stomach was much larger than I remembered, she had a flower tucked into her hair and had fashioned a rough skirt and shirt from grasses and plants. Lucifer had changed as well, he had taken a truly human form, complete with what was needed to mate with Lillith. He was still one of us, still had his power but it seemed somehow muted within him.

I forced myself to remain civil, "Lillith. It is lovely to see you again. What is this you have on?"

"It helps keep the biting things off of me," she replied. "And the sun when it is hot. Neither of those things seem to bother Lucifer though." A shade of guilt crossed her face but she continued explaining why she was clothed, "I wanted to be more colorful as well, like the birds," She smiled, "They have always been my favorite thing you created. How long are you staying? We have both missed you." One of her arms casually wrapped around Lucifer's waist and he briefly leaned into her.

"I am not sure. It appears there are many things that have happened while I have been away."

Lucifer caught my meaning as did Lillith who placed her other hand on her stomach. She looked up at him, then back at me. "Do not be angry Remiel, please," she pleaded.

Lucifer removed her arm from his waist and stepped away, "Perhaps Remiel and I should speak first. We will be back soon." He walked past me a few steps and waited. "Remiel, I know you do not owe me or us a hearing." he said softly, "Once all of you left I accepted that I would never see any of you again."

I took a few moments to try to understand what that would be like for him. He and Lillith were bonded so completely and with Adam's new mate taking Lillith's place at his side it should not have shocked me that this had occurred. I tried to set aside what I was feeling as I joined him. He looked at me and I gestured that he should lead the way. Gold eyes captured mine as a small, nervous grin brought a slight curve to his mouth.

"How has Elohim not hurt you in this form?"

"This? This is merely a shell. I am still as I was. He has tried, failed and returned to that forest to accept Adam and Eve's adulation. At least he did until he cast them out."

I was not entirely sure coming back had been the best idea. I was certainly not up to these many shocks all at once, "What? Why? What did you do?"

He laughed, it was a rather bitter sounding one, "I had little to do with it. It appears Eve likes to explore the world around her and had somehow evaded the guardians who were supposed to keep her from tainting. She saw Lillith weaving those garments she wears. Lillith spotted Eve hiding in the bushes, shaking in fear while wanting to learn and invited her closer."

"You never informed Lillith to avoid Eve?"

"Why would I do that?" he asked, "After I corrupted his winged thing Elohim took them all deep into those woods. He made more of the winged ones, which I entertained myself by turning against him for some time," he paused and looked around. Then bent over and plucked a plant from the ground. "She likes to eat the root from these. For some time I kept quite a distance away from Lillith. I felt that it was best in case he ever created something that was an actual threat to me. I did not want her to get caught in the midst of a battle. After several years it appeared that all he truly cared about was having things worship him, praise him and endlessly thank him for creating them.

Adam and Eve as well as those winged things were wholly under his control and he seemed content with that. I grew tired of watching it so chose to spend more time with Lillith. In all the years I had watched them Eve had never strayed far from Adam or Elohim and I would never put limits on what Lillith could and could not do. It seems that Eve grew tired of the endless worship of Elohim and went looking for adventure. That's when she found Lillith. It was as I told him from the beginning, you cannot force love. It must be given and earned. Lillith taught Eve, who returned with her new skills to Adam. I knew the moment Elohim had spotted Eve wearing her garments. A rather large amount of trees shattered in the deepest part of the woods." His nervous grin from earlier was replaced by something much more sinister and cold. "He shouted my name and came for me. See those mountains in the distance?" He pointed off to the east. "They used to be much taller. I destroyed several of his guardians and our battle lasted several days."

154

"You two fought and we did not sense it? How?" The two of them battling for days should have ripped the world apart.

"Elohim knows that if all of you were to get involved it would not go well for him. We hid ourselves from you as we battled and both of us chose to not do anything too destructive. He threatened Lillith several times during those days, then something happened." He stopped walking and turned to face me with a guarded expression. "She hid herself from him, somehow she discovered a way to manipulate the energy around her. Perhaps she has seen me do it so many times while I transported her from place to place that she learned how. When she did that he flew into an even greater rage, which is when those mountains were almost destroyed. Then he returned to where Adam and Eve were, cast them out and charged his winged guardians to keep them out. Lillith feels as if she is to blame for their misfortune. She tried to help them afterwards but Adam chased her away, blaming her and Eve for destroying what had been perfect. Since then she has avoided them. They are off to the west somewhere."

He stopped speaking, "And the rest?" I asked, too numb from everything he had said so far to really form any actual thoughts.

"Yes, the rest," he took a deep breath before he continued. "When she hid herself from Elohim, I had to acknowledge that what I gifted her with had made her something much beyond what she had been intended to be. You are already aware of how I feel towards her. Once the battle with Elohim was over and he had cast out Adam and Eve she came to me and asked if we were truly all that different. She had seen the winged things Elohim created, felt my pain when we battled and hid herself from both Elohim and his guardians." He looked away from me, back towards the direction we had come from, back to her. "She pointed out that her teaching Eve had resulted in a similar outcome as my teaching of her did. Neither of us meant harm, but intentions and outcomes are rarely linked together it seems. I told her that I fully intended to corrupt anything Elohim would make and she stated that she believed as I did, that no living thing should be controlled by

155

another. It was at that moment that I created this shell." He gestured towards his much more human self.

I was barely able to form words, "Her offspring Lucifer, your offspring. Have you given no thought to them? Do you even know what they will be? What they will be capable of?"

"How would I know such things Remiel?" His eyes returned to mine, there was no shame, no regret in them. Just resolve. "Elohim no longer brings creations to life. Our original calling is truly meaningless without that. You feel it. I can see it in your face, feel it within you. Yet life still goes on, does it not? The universe still functions, still grows, still breathes. In this form, with this shell, she and I can create something still. Something unique and beautiful. Do you understand?"

I wanted to feel anger and hatred towards him. He had broken every boundary there was, even more than Elohim had, but I could not, because he was right. I felt adrift, meaningless and lost without being able to truly create something. Yes, I could still shape worlds, but life, to create something and then watch it stir, take it's first breath and grow. That I could no longer do, none of us could. Yet Lucifer had found a way and who was I to condemn him for it.

"Yes, I do," I eventually replied, "Although I know I shouldn't."

His form slowly changed back into his original walking about form and a hint of his aura rippled around him, "Will you tell the others?" he asked. His tone was not threatening but the fact that he was abandoning the more human shell was.

I was so weary of fighting, "I am tired of battles Lucifer. Tired of questions that have no safe answers, tired of losing things I have cared for. I will say nothing. If they return here and find out it is between you and them. Do not thank me. I do not do this for you."

He nodded, "Of course Remiel, I understand." He shifted back to the more human shell and we returned to Lillith. I spent the rest of

156

the day and well into the night with them. Lillith attempted to bring up the incident with Eve once or twice in an effort to ask my forgiveness for some obscure reason. I simply told her that what happened between all of them was something I chose not to get involved with anymore. Once they both realized that I was not there to judge their moods shifted into something much more relaxed. Lucifer frequently smiled at things she said or did and she returned his affections quite enthusiastically.

After she fell asleep I sent one last thought to Lucifer, "It has been good to see you smile again brother, no matter the reason why. I must leave now." I really had no pressing thing to do but the sight of them, their happiness and joy was raising even more confusion in my mind, more unanswerable questions that began to weigh heavily upon me.

He stood, crossed the few steps that were between us and engulfed me in a tight embrace, not just with his arms but with his entire being. "You requested that I not thank you," he whispered to me, "and I shan't. It was good to see you again. Farewell."

He stepped back and I left before anything else could unsettle me further.

Was Lucifer truly wrong in what he did? Perhaps, perhaps not. The stories of their offspring have been changed, just as his. Those humans who can trace their lineage back to Lillith and Lucifer, they are the ones who have hints of power that no science can explain. They know things, feel a greater connection to something they cannot describe. I have seen it bring them great joy and great pain.

Elohim has told his side of the story, how he views the events that happened. Is there truth in it? Of course, there is some truth in all stories. My truth is perhaps more subtle, my story more hidden. I chose a different path, a more neutral path. I was given the name Seeker, Teacher, Hermit by humans. I found my own form of joy. Perhaps one day I will share it with you, but for now I have

157

someone awaiting me and have perchance shared more truth than was wise.

I leave you with this final thought, "As a matter of honor, one man owes it to another to manifest the truth."~ Thomas Aquinas

   -Remiel.